RIDE THE STORM

SHARON KIZZIAH-HOLMES

Book Design – Sharon Kizziah-Holmes

Paperback-Press
an imprint of A & S Publishing
Paperback Press, LLC
Springfield, Missouri

ISBN -13: 978-1-970560-06-0

DEDICATION

Husband, you have supported my goals throughout our 46 the years together, in music and writing. The first time I saw you, I knew you, who picks a mean guitar, wears the hell out of blue jeans and a cowboy hat, were the one

I love you, D man.

ACKNOWLEDGMENTS

Where do I start? There are so many to thank.

Ozarks Romance Authors members have been by my side for over 30 years. You've are friends, mentors, writing partners, and the list goes on. Thank you for your support.

Writers of the Purple Page is a group of writers who do many things together, including public speaking...and lunch. Kathy, Susan, Shirley, Conetta, Tierney and Lois, I enjoy our daily banter over morning coffee, sharing personal woes, triumphs, heartbreaks and happy events. The messages we share about writing, events and learning experiences are inspiring, but most of all I cherish our bond and friendship.

Critique me Friday, I'm honored to be a founding member of this awesome critique group. John, Shirley, Michael, Lori, Conetta, David and Heather Burch, may she rest in peace. I know I don't bring much writing to the table anymore, but I sure do have fun critiquing y'all's. (I love my red pen.) You guys make every Friday something to look forward to. The comradery we have is priceless. It's funny how, in a great critique group like ours, we can be honest, tear each other's writing down, only for the author to build back up as a better, stronger read. Six years is a long time for a critique group to stick together. That's a sign we appreciate each other and value the opinions of our friends/members. Thank you for letting me be a part.

Clarissa, thank you for becoming a close friend, and helping to make me an award winning book designer. We make a good team.

Most of all, to the Creator, thank You for blessing me in so many ways.

ACKNOWLEDGMENTS

PROLOGUE

R ain raised her hand and waved to the applauding audience. "Thank you. Thank you so much." She took a seat on a stool that sat in the middle of the stage. "Now I'd like to sing a song for a special friend." She looked directly at the cowboy in the front row. The same seat he'd occupied for her last ten performances. "I think you know who you are."

Their gazes met. The first time she saw him, she felt she'd looked into those eyes before. Now, as Luke's gray eyes sparkled in the dim light, the thought occurred to her again. A sensual grin lifted the corners of his mouth. He kindly nodded his head.

Her heart raced with the want for the tall, mysterious cowboy. "This one's called, Ride the Storm." The band started the musical introduction. Rain's body heat escalated when Luke gave her a simple wink. She couldn't understand how he aroused her so easily.

Knowing this could be the last song in the show, and it was especially for Luke, she put her all into it. She'd been playing Vegas for two weeks and tonight would bring an end to the engagement. Tomorrow, on to Reno.

"…The Stoorrmm..." She held the last note until her lungs were empty. She bowed to her fans and made her way backstage. The thunderous sound of appreciation continued long enough to warrant a curtain call.

After she appeased her audience with another song, she headed to her dressing room. The moment she entered a sweet aroma assailed her senses. A beautiful bouquet of yellow roses decorated the table in the middle of the small cubical. She smiled, crossed the short area and retrieved the attached envelope. The message written on the card inside warmed her heart. "A rose for a rose."

At that moment, Rain made up her mind. For two weeks she'd pondered the idea of letting Luke into her bed and her life. They met the first day she came to town. He hadn't put any fast moves on her like most of the men, who thought she was a star. He'd remained the perfect gentleman. Her past haunted her and she had stayed away from serious relationships, but Luke was different.

A knock sounded at her dressing room door. "Who is it?" She heard a smooth deep voice resound from the other side.

"It's Luke."

Her palms grew sticky. She glanced in the mirror and a flush colored her cheeks. "Just a minute." She rushed to change from her stage clothes into her jeans. When she opened the door, her heart threatened to stop at the sight of him.

His six-foot two-inch frame stood leisurely in the hallway. Silver-belly Stetson in hand, his brown hair shone with sun-streaked highlights. Steel gray eyes peered into her soul.

"May I come in?"

"Of course." She could see his sinewy muscles at work underneath his tight fitting clothing as he entered. "Have a seat."

"Thanks." He sat on a chair in a corner.

"No, thank *you*. For the roses." She walked to the vase and gently caressed a bud. "They're beautiful." She could hardly bring herself to meet his gaze. The heat his look caused in her, kindled a fire too intense to ignore. She decided now was as good a time as any, to ask her question. A question she had never asked any other man. She nervously cleared her throat. "Luke?"

"Yes."

"What would you...do you...would you spend the night with me?" She heard him rise from his chair. When he reached her side, the warmth of his body made her shiver. His closeness caused her to feel as if her heart would beat its way through her chest. From the corner of her eye she saw him set his hat on the dressing table.

He placed a finger under her chin and forced her to meet his gaze. "Look me in the eye and ask me that."

Her skin seared beneath his touch and air rush in and out of her lungs, her breath came in short sporadic spurts. She had to have him. Her voice escaped just above a whisper. "Stay with me tonight, Luke."

Sunrays peeked through the window of the plush motel room and awakened Rain. She glanced over at the man that lay beside her. Luke's shoulder-length hair was tousled from sleep. His mustache, neatly trimmed, curved around the corners of his full lips.

She recalled the first night she saw him sitting in the front row of the audience. His eyes danced with admiration for her. During the show he held his silver-belly cowboy hat in his lap, then afterward proudly placed it back on his head. His jeans were crisply pressed and his western shirt hugged his muscular build. She knew she had to meet the handsome man.

Never before had she felt so drawn to someone, but there was something about his eyes. Somehow, they told her he was unlike any man she'd ever known. Maybe she could trust him. Now she lay beside him after a night of passion.

Luke's eyes fluttered open. "Mmm, good morning, Rain." He took her into his arms. "You look beautiful this morning. How do you feel?"

"Wonderful."

His finger traced her bare skin. "I agree."

She touched his face with her fingertips and heard the seriousness in her own voice when she spoke. "Will I ever hear from you again, Mr. Dilashaw?" The look on his face told the story, but she didn't understand.

He released her and swung his feet off the bed onto the floor. "Our paths might cross someday."

Her heart sank. Had her intuitions been wrong? Was this only a one-night stand to him? "When?"

"Don't ask me that, Rain. I can't answer."

"I'm not asking for a lifetime commitment, only a phone call." Why was he acting this way?

Luke stood, pulled on his jeans and fastened his belt. He turned to face her. "Look, it was nice to have met you. Last night...well, last night was wonderful, but I can't make promises."

Rain sat up in bed and clutched the covers. "Did I say anything about promises?" She felt she would be sick. Why had his demeanor changed so abruptly?

He put on his shirt and fingered the buttons through the holes. "Let's not argue. What we've shared the last couple of weeks has been great. Let's leave it at that and make it a good memory." He sat in the chair beside the bed and pulled on his boots. "I'd better be going."

She wouldn't allow herself to be hurt by this man. "Yes, I guess you'd better." She watched as he put his hand on the doorknob.

Luke fought the urge to go to Rain, take her in his arms and tell her the truth. That he wanted to be with her. But he couldn't. He hated himself for letting it go this far, but she was more than he could resist.

Looking at her now, the contrast of her dark skin against the white sheets made the Native American half of her heritage apparent. Her long black hair hung over her shoulders. She was beautiful. He could tell she was trying to hide the hurt he had caused, but her light chestnut-colored eyes deceived her effort.

"Good-bye, Rain." His heart plummeted when he opened the door. He couldn't look back, as much as he wanted to, he couldn't.

CHAPTER 1

"Fifteen minutes 'til show time, Miss Storm."

"Thanks." Rain shuffled through the contents in her bag. In a few minutes she would do her last performance at this job. She wanted to make sure she'd gathered everything that belonged to her from the dressing room.

She spotted a small white envelope in the bottom of the bag. Hesitantly, she reached for it. As she read the five simple words written on the card inside, her mind traced back through the months to the day she received it. Memories of his betrayal flooded her senses and she wondered how she had ever thought she could trust Luke Dilashaw with her heart.

"Miss Storm?"

Wanting never to be reminded of him again, she ripped the card into tiny pieces and tossed it away. "Yes."

"Ten minutes 'til show time."

"Thank you. I'll be right there."

Rain checked her appearance one last time then started for the door when her cell phone rang. She swiped her finger across the screen. "Hello."

"Sammi? Is that you?"

She recognized the voice. No one but her mom, and

the people from home, called her by her given name. A smile crossed her lips. "Yes, Momma, it's me."

"How are you, honey?"

"Fine, Mrs. Rainwater, and you?"

"Oh, why do you always call me that?"

"Because I never get to hear my real name unless I talk to you."

"Samantha Rainwater, you're silly. Did you hear your name then?"

She smiled. "Yes. Thank you, Momma."

"Honey, listen, I have bad news."

Samantha's pulse quickened. "Are you okay?"

"It's Howard...his heart again." She paused. "It's bad this time. Doc says he's dying, Sam."

Samantha took a seat on the chair. "Oh, no." The man had hired her mother as a live-in housekeeper over twenty years ago. Samantha had grown to love him like a father. "What happened?"

"Well, you know how he is about thinking he's the only one who can break a horse on this ranch. I couldn't stop him, and his old heart wouldn't take it. The doctor says it's just a matter of time."

"He's not even sixty yet. That's too young to die." Her heart broke.

"I know, baby girl."

A muffled voice came through the door. "Five minutes, Miss Storm."

"Momma, I have to go. I'll call you back when the show's over."

"Sam, he's asking for you."

Tears threatened to spill from her eyes. "I'll make arrangements to come home."

"Thank you, baby girl. You don't have to call back."

"Okay. I'll see you soon." She swiped the red end call button.

Samantha's mind spun and she blinked back tears. It

was imperative she get herself together. The show must go on. She once again assumed the role of Rain Storm and forced herself to perform as if nothing was wrong.

The beautiful spring day did nothing to boost Samantha's spirits. The longest part of her journey behind her, she had only twenty more miles to go. She whisked her windblown hair back, stopped her red Mustang convertible at a traffic light in the town of Elko, Nevada and studied the familiar surroundings.

She'd spent lots of time here when she was growing up. Her destination today was Lamoille, Nevada and the H-H spread where Howard Hale lay ill. She had lived at the H-H since her mother took the job on the ranch. Her unhappy childhood in Oklahoma was a far cry from the beauty of the Nevada hills.

While she was stopped, she decided to call her mom on the H-H landline. On the third ring, someone picked up.

"Hello."

She didn't recognize the woman's voice. "Hi, is this the Hale residence?"

"Yes, ma'am, I'm one of the nurses helping to care for Mr. Hale."

"This is Samantha Rainwater. I'm on my way there. Is everything okay?"

"It's as good as it can be, ma'am. Mrs. Rainwater is with Howard now, so she asked me to answer."

Her mind eased a little. She feared her mother had pushed herself too hard and may have also fallen ill. "Great. Would you tell her I'll be there in twenty minutes, please?"

The light turned green as she hung up. She made the turn onto the road that would lead her to Spring Creek and through Lamoille Canyon.

Glancing out the window to her right, she saw Goldtown Hotel and Casino. Across the block stood another casino, the Bigbear. To her left, on the corner, was Steelman's western wear. She'd bought her first stage outfit there. Continuing through town, she began her final leg home.

Lamoille Canyon was a beautiful sight and brought back many pleasant memories. As she drove through the tiny town of Lamoille, where Main Street was less than two blocks long, a smile crossed her face at the sight of Idaloo's bar. "I've played and sang many a song in there," she said to the wind.

It took only moments to pass through town. Trees covered the road and spring wildflowers dotted the pastures. May was a beautiful time of year, and she hated to return home for such a sad occasion.

Ahead, she saw the marker that bore the symbol of the H-H ranch. It announced the beginning of the large spread.

Most people in the area raised cattle. Not Howard Hale, he loved horses. Howard owned numerous breeds, but his favorite was the quarter horse.

Samantha pulled onto the lane that led to the ranch house. Oh, how she loved this place. She glanced overhead as she passed under the big, iron prototype of the H-H brand. She'd seen it thousands of times, but each time she smiled at its beauty.

Halfway down the lane she braked the Mustang to a stop and marveled at the sight atop the hill. Trees filled the yard of the two-story, hand-crafted log home, and a rail fence held its borders, with sage covered hills as the backdrop. Four small outbuildings, a bunkhouse, a large barn and three corrals, dotted with horses, supplied the final touches to the majestic scene.

She loved this ranch and was grateful to have had the chance to grow up surrounded by such loveliness. It was her favorite place to be.

Longing for the natural peace and quiet of the place, she picked up her cell phone then turned it off. There was no decent reception in the area anyway, so she very seldom used it here. Its silence was a welcome reprieve from agent calls, booking calls, spam etc.

Everyone knew if they wanted to get hold of her while she was at the ranch, they'd have to call the house phone, which they never did because she seldom took the calls anyway. It may have been rude, but sometimes she had to have downtime. "Freedom," she whispered then pressed the gas pedal once again. She pulled into the circle drive and turned off the ignition.

"Sammi!"

She glanced in the rear-view mirror and saw the image of a woman coming toward the car. A smile lifted her lips. "Momma," she whispered, then opened the door and stepped out.

Lena Rainwater was full blood Cherokee. Her dark complexion brought out the gray in her once black hair.

"Sammi, I'm glad you're here."

Samantha greeted her mother with a hug. The safety she'd grown accustomed to as a child, while encircled in her mother's arms, overwhelmed her and covered her in warmth. "Me too, Momma."

She slipped her arm through her mother's and strolled through the park-like yard. Samantha glanced down at Lena's five-foot-three frame. "How's Howard?"

"He's resting right now, but his condition worsened during the night. The doctor thinks he had another heart attack."

"Why hasn't he gone to the hospital in Elko?"

"He refuses to leave the ranch. Says he knows his life on earth is over, and he's going to meet the Lord from his own bedroom."

She caught her breath and fought the tears that welled in her eyes. "Sounds like Howard."

They approached a set of wooden Adirondack chairs placed around a table nestled beneath a large tree. Lena took a seat. "Sit down, honey, let's talk."

She sat opposite her mother and noted the tired expression on the older woman's face. "Mom, have you had any rest?"

"A little. I've been working with the nurses to try to keep Howard comfortable. You know how demanding he can be."

Samantha smiled and nodded. He acted like a gruff guy, but she knew he was really a teddy bear.

"I want to talk about you, Sam. Have your bad dreams stopped?"

The reoccurring nightmare that had plagued her since childhood flashed in her mind. "It's been months since I've had one."

"I'm glad to hear that. I owe my life to you, baby girl."

Her heart dropped to her stomach. "Oh, Momma, let's not talk about it."

"You know the doctor said the more you bring your fears into the open, the sooner you'll get over—"

"Momma…" She shook her head. The vision of a raging rainstorm flashed in her mind. She didn't want to think about it now. "Please."

"Okay, Sam. You've suffered way more than I have since that night twenty years ago."

Lena rose, came around to her daughter's side and placed a hand on her shoulder. "I'd better go in and check on things. Are you ready?"

She patted her mother's tiny hand. "I think I'll sit here a while. Call me when Howard wakes up."

"I'm sorry I brought this up so soon after you arrived."

"Don't worry about it, Momma. I'm all grown up now. I can take it." All the woman was trying to do was help her push the memories aside, but every time it was brought up, they came rushing back. Her mother would never mention that fateful event if she knew it actually hurt her more after talking about it, and she would never tell her.

Lena bent and kissed Samantha atop the head. "I love you."

"I love you, too." She watched her mother disappear into the house, then turned to scan the hillside.

What was going to happen to the ranch now? With the old man gone, it would leave his younger brother to take over. Johnny Hale was Howard's only known relative.

Johnny was a nice enough man, she supposed. He'd been foreman over the ranch hands for the last few years. After doing time in prison for armed robbery, Johnny had no place to go, so Howard took him in and taught him the horse ranching business. Some years passed before Howard granted him the position. Sometimes he could be harsh but he knew how to make the hands get the work done.

Samantha remembered overhearing Howard on an occasion when he warned Johnny not to anger the help. He'd told the man, 'Our employees are our number one priority. They are the backbone of the ranch, and we have to take care of them, Johnny, remember that'.

"Sam."

She glanced up at the sound of her mother's call.

"Howard's asking for you."

Leaving the pleasant setting, she ran to the house. A lump formed in her throat as she followed her mother.

When they entered the doorway of Howard's bedroom, the distinct odor of medication invaded her nostrils. She glanced around. Everything looked the same except a hospital bed now occupied the space where Howard's favorite king-size bed once was. Between the covers lay a man that still exuded the air of power. Wires trailed from his chest to monitors placed next to the bed, and a nurse stood watch.

Howard held out his hand. "Sammi, come see me."

Her concern deepened at the ashen color of his skin.

"You've got it, Howie." She approached the side rail of the bed, leaned down and placed her arms around his neck. Weakness radiated through his embrace. She straightened and grasped his chilled hand. "You look like crap."

Laughter escaped his throat. "Finally, someone who will be honest with me. You're a sight for sore eyes, girl."

She brushed tendrils of white hair from his forehead. "Thanks. What were you trying to prove by breaking a horse, you old fart? You haven't done that in years."

"Hey, I'm not that old. And watch your tongue, there are ladies present." He gestured toward her mother and the nurse. "Would you two mind stepping out to give me and Sammi some time alone?"

The nurse glanced at her watch. "Only a few minutes. It's almost time for your medication."

"To hell with that! I'll holler when I'm ready for you to come back. Now, scoot on out of here."

Samantha watched a smile cross her mother's face as she followed the nurse out the door. She pulled a nearby chair closer to the bed. "A little rough on her, weren't you?"

"I'm tired of this, Sam. I wish the Lord would lead me to the pearly gates so I could rest."

"I'm not sure He'll want you, as crabby as you are."

"Oh, but when I meet St. Peter, all will be well."

She nodded her understanding.

"Raise the head of the bed, would you?"

After pushing the button on the bed rail, she helped him get situated, then took her seat. "What's on your mind, old man?"

"Samantha, I have something to tell you. First of all, I love you. You're like a daughter to me, and I appreciate your mother sharing you with me all these years."

"Howard—"

"Now, let me talk, before I get too weak."

She sat back and granted his wish. "Okay."

"Sam, I've kept something from you all these years. Something very important, to me at least. I—I have an heir."

She gazed into his faded gray eyes and saw a twinkle of happiness she'd never seen before and smiled. "You have a child?"

"Yes. A son."

"No kidding?" She watched a disgusted frown crease his brow.

"Now, Sam, why would I kid about something like this?"

She placed a comforting hand on his arm. "Don't get your dander up. I was only teasing. Have you ever seen him?"

"I met him about six months ago." Lost in thought, he gazed at the ceiling for a long while.

She spoke to pull him from his trance-like state. "Howard?"

He smiled into the air. "Oh, what a sight he was. I tried to contact him through the years, but his mother and her husband kept us apart. Then, when his step-father died, my ex-wife thought my son should know his real daddy."

"I never knew you were married."

"Not many people did. We married young. I can't understand why she married me. She hated the fact I was a cowboy and that I loved the cowboy way of life."

"Maybe she was in love and that came with the package."

"Maybe, but... Anyway back then the ranch was nothing like it is today. Hell, we lived in a little trailer. Half the time the bathroom didn't work. Thankfully there was an old outhouse we could use. It was pretty disgusting, but we got by."

"What happened between you two?"

"I cheated on her. I was riding the rodeo circuit. She was pregnant and couldn't go on the road with me. Alone most of the time, I became lonely."

Samantha thought of her own life on the road as a country singer. It was lonely. Everyone thought Rain Storm was a happy, well-rounded person, when actually she needed a lifetime partner.

"I had a couple of women. They didn't mean anything but sexual release. I thought of Linda. Day and night she was on my mind. I decided the Elko rodeo would be my last. Jack Daniel's got the best of me and I forgot where I was. I took a girl to a local motel and that's when Linda showed up at the door.

"Howard, you don't have to tell me anymore. I understand."

"Yeah, well, I need to talk about it. She moved to Santa Fe, New Mexico. I missed her with all my heart and soul. I tried desperately to get her to come back, but she never liked 'life on the farm' as she called it. She filed for divorce. I didn't protest.

"After she left, I bought my first horses. Soon, I began to make money. I bought, sold and traded. In a few years I learned about breeding. Made enough to build this house." He studied the large master bedroom. "I love this place, Sam."

The old man appeared exhausted. "Howard, why don't you rest? You look tired."

"I am tired, child, but I want to talk. I finally have a friend in my presence."

"I thought my mother was your friend."

"Your mother *is* my friend, Sam. I told her about this years ago. I made her promise never to tell a soul."

Samantha fidgeted her hands together. "Howard." Her pulse jumped with anticipation. She had wanted to ask this question for years. "Have you and my mother..." She paused. "Well, you know."

"Yes, I know, and no we haven't." He crossed his arms over his chest. "Why would you ask such a thing?"

"I don't know. I guess I just wished someone like you could have been *my* father."

"Even after what I've just stated?"

She met his questioning gaze. "You're a kind, generous man. Like you said, you were young when all that happened. You did the best you could in life."

Tears streamed down his face. "Like I told you, I tried to see my son."

Her brow furrowed at the hurt in his eyes.

"Year upon year I wrote him letters, only to get them back in the mail marked, return to sender. When I went to Santa Fe and tried to see him, Linda and her husband had me arrested for trespassing. Shortly after that, I gave up all rights and agreed to let Linda's husband adopt him.

"Does your son know you're sick?"

Howard nodded. "Yes, he knows. I actually contacted after my first heart attack six or so months ago." He addressed her solemnly. "Sam, I'm going to leave the place to him." He wiped his cheek with his hand. "It's in my will that your mother keeps her job until she can no longer do it. Then she's to be taken care of for the rest of her life."

Samantha breathed a sigh of relief. "Thank you. I've worried about that."

"Well don't. I know you've made some money as a singer, but you can't support your mother. I can. Or, now, my son can. And, Samantha, you know that little valley on the south end you love so much?"

She thought of the beautiful site and the small pond that rested in the center. "Yes."

"It's yours."

Having a home on that piece of property had always been a dream of hers. She jumped to her feet and hugged him. "Oh, Howard, thank you, but you don't have to give me anything. You've provided me with enough in my life."

He lovingly pushed her away. "Don't fuss with me girl. It's already done."

If there were any piece of land in the world she would want, that was it. "Okay, Howie." She didn't want to upset him by arguing. "What about Johnny? Won't he be ticked?"

Howard shook his head. "I'll leave my son to deal with my brother, but I've taken care of him, too."

"Shouldn't you bring your son to the ranch?"

"I had your mother call him right after this little episode took place."."

She blinked several times. The shock of his words settled over her. "He's here?"

"Yes. I asked your mother not to say anything until I got a chance to explain."

Her blood rushed with expectation of meeting the son of Howard Hale. "Where is he?"

"I sent him into town to take care of some legal business."

She glanced out the window. "The sun's going down. He'll probably be back soon."

"Well, right now I'm hungry. Call in the cook."

"Now, Howard, you know Mother doesn't like it when you call her 'the cook'."

"She cooks for me, doesn't she?"

"Yes, she does but—"

"Then she should learn not to be so sensitive."

"You old bear. One of these days she's going to skin you."

A knock sounded at the door. Howard continued his gruff demure. "What?"

A deep voice came from the other side. "I'm back, Dad, may I come in?"

The old man glanced over at her, raised his eyebrows and smiled. "Yes. Come in."

Samantha thought the voice sounded familiar and her heart threatened to stop when the door swung open. Her knees shook and she caught hold of the end of the bed. She could barely breathe but forced out his name in a whisper. "Luke."

CHAPTER 2

L uke couldn't believe his eyes. It was really her. "Rain? What are you doing here?" She let go of the footboard and straightened. He could tell she was trying to compose herself. She wasn't the only one shaken by this encounter. He tried to slow his racing heart.

"I live here."

He drew a long breath and held it. She was even more beautiful than he remembered. He forced back the ache in his arms to hold her. Dreams of seeing her again had plagued him, but never in his wildest illusions did he think it would be here. He glanced at his father and swallowed hard. "She lives here?"

"I told you about her. This is Samantha."

Luke's gaze shifted to meet Samantha's. "You're Samantha Rainwater? I thought your name was Rain Storm."

"That's my stage name."

Howard cleared his throat. "You two know each other?"

Samantha placed her hands on her hips. "Unfortunately, yes. We met in...Vegas, wasn't it?"

Her sarcasm got to him. She knew damn good and well it was Las Vegas "You know it was Vegas, Rain. I—"

"My. Name. Is. Samantha!"

Luke duly noted her hateful tone. He didn't blame her for being bitter, but this was over and above hateful. With everything that was going on in his life right now, he refused to put up with her acid tongue. "Let's go somewhere else. I think you and I need to talk."

"Anything you have to say to me, Howard is welcome to hear."

Luke went to Samantha's side and gripped her upper arm. "In private." He saw the amused smile on Howard's face and could imagine what he was thinking. He turned to leave and addressed the old man. "Excuse us for a moment." He could swear he heard his father mumble something about 'sparks' as he escorted Rain from the bedroom.

Samantha's flesh burned at each point Luke's fingers came into contact. She struggled against his grasp. "Let me go." Her gaze met her mother's as they passed in the hallway. "Momma?"

Luke tilted his cowboy hat toward Lena. "Ma'am."

Samantha thought for sure the sight of her mother would make him release his hold, but he continued through the house and out the door. She glanced back to see if Lena followed. She didn't. This was ridiculous. She felt like a little girl being taken to the principal's office. "Luke, you'd better..."

When Luke let her go, she turned to face him. Her heart hit her chest wall as though it was going to break free. Instinctively, her hand flew through the air and met the side of his face. The sound of a sharp smack echoed against the hills. "Don't ever touch me again." she growled through gritted teeth.

He raised his hand to his cheek, and she saw a glint of amusement twinkle in his eyes. Of all the nerve. Samantha fought to control her temper. Memories of her reoccurring nightmare flooded her mind. "I'm warning you. Stay away from me." He stepped toward her and reached for her shoulders, but she jerked away.

"Please, Rain, let's talk."

"Again, my name is Samantha." His somber eyes penetrated her soul. Her mind flashed back to the first time she saw him. In Vegas she could have sworn she'd looked into those eyes before, now she knew why. They were a younger version of Howard Hale's eyes. She turned away. "I don't have anything to say to you." When he stepped up behind her, his breath fanned her hair, causing her to shiver against the warm evening air.

"Well, I have something to say to you."

She glanced at the orange glow of the sunset as it sank behind the western hills. She longed to seek comfort in Luke's arms, but that was absurd. "I'm sure it's nothing I want to hear." She turned and ran.

The door leading into the house seemed miles away. Once she entered, she pursued the safety of her room. She slammed the door then fell onto the bed and cried herself to sleep.

Late in the evening, Luke answered his father's request to return to his bedside. "I'm sorry about that little scene earlier, Dad."

Howard smiled. "I'm not. It's about time we had some life in this house. Since Sammi left it's been boring around here. So tell me, what's going on between you two?"

Luke had grown to respect his father over the last few months and found it easy to talk to him. "I don't want to burden you with it."

"Oh, hell, boy, give an old man something to think about besides dying."

Luke smiled. "Alright, you asked for it." He sat back

and memories washed over his mind. "Just after mother told me about you, I decided to take a vacation. I needed to gather my thoughts. Vegas sounded like the perfect place.

"Marquees flashed from all sides, but the one at Pharaoh's caught my eye. When I saw Rain Storm was appearing, I turned in and got a room.

"I'd seen her years earlier when she performed at a rodeo I was riding in. Her dark hair shone in the arena lights and her voice rang out for miles. I had a girlfriend hanging on my arm or I would have attempted to meet her then.

"Anyway, I got a front row seat for her show at Pharaoh's. In a short time we struck up a friendship and before I knew it, the two weeks were over. The last night, she asked me—"

A horrible scream penetrated the walls. Luke recognized Samantha's voice and stood. His heart jumped to his throat. "What the hell?" He lunged for the door.

"Stop! Please, stop! Mommaaaa!" she cried.

Luke followed the sound. His blood ran cold when he heard her terrified scream again. When he reached her bedroom door, he burst in expecting a confrontation with an intruder. He flipped on the light switch. Samantha lay alone, her body curled into a ball, tears streaming down her face. Her eyes were open but she had a faraway look like she wasn't really seeing what was around her.. He rushed to her side.

Beads of sweat rolled from her brow. "I killed him."

Luke shushed her. "It's okay, it was only a dream." He took a seat on the bed and cradled her in his arms. The sudden urge to protect her, from whatever fears she had, consumed him. "You're fine, Sam, I'll take care of you." She clung to him like a child. Her breathing labored, she sobbed into his chest. It felt so natural to hold her. Comfort her.

"I killed him."

"No, it was a nightmare." Luke heard someone coming down the hall.

Lena stepped through the open doorway. "Honey? Are you alright?"

"She had a bad dream." The look of concern on Lena's face tore at his heart.

"Yes, I know."

Samantha raised her head. "Momma? Is that you?"

"It's me, baby girl."

She focused on Luke and pushed away. "What are you doing here?"

Her tear-stained face tore at his heart. The last thing he wanted to do was leave her, but he stood. "I heard you scream and thought you might be in danger. Are you okay?" Her gaze softened and he hoped she'd ask him to stay.

Tears flowed steadily down her cheeks. "Yes, I'm okay. Now please, leave."

Luke ached to comfort her, but apparently it wasn't what *she* wanted. He placed a finger under her chin and forced her to meet his gaze. Pain from deep within caused dullness to cloud her brandy-colored eyes. More than anything, he wanted to kiss her troubles away, take her into his arms and hold her for a lifetime, but that wasn't possible. With his thumb, he wiped a tear drop from her cheek then took his leave.

Samantha's face tingled where Luke had touched it. She watched him walk out of her bedroom and fought the desire to run after him. She grabbed the door, slammed it shut then turned toward Lena. "Oh, Momma." Though Samantha towered inches over the little woman, she was comforted by her caress.

"I know. I know. I'm sorry you had another nightmare."

"Are they ever going to end?"

"They will, honey. One day they will."

Samantha sniffed and stepped away. "It was as clear as if it just happened." She walked over and took a seat on the bed.

Lena followed. "Feel like talking about it now?"

She shook her head. "You don't want to hear it again." Her mother took a seat beside her and placed a comforting arm around her shoulders.

"I'll listen to it a million times if it makes you feel better."

Maybe it would help her to recall her dream out loud. She closed her eyes and went back to the dream and the memory. "The thunder's roaring and lightning's flashing. I can hear the rain beating down on the metal roof of the trailer house. I get out of my bed and sneak into your room. I don't know if daddy's there or not.

In the safety of her mother's arms, Samantha regressed. She was once again a six-year-old reliving that horrible night twenty years ago.

⸏⸏◦∽⸏

"Are you scared of the storm, baby girl?"

"Yes, Mommy. Are you by yourself?"

"Uh-huh."

"Can I sleep with you?"

"Of course you can, Sammi."

"I'm sorry I'm scared, Mommy."

"It's alright for little girls to be scared of storms, especially a rainstorm as bad as this one."

"Mommy, when I grow up will I still be afraid?"

Lena cuddled her six-year-old child in her arms. "I don't think so."

"Good."

"Where the hell are you?!"

It was her father's voice. Samantha heard a loud crash come from the living room. She couldn't stop breathing fast. Pulling the covers up to her chin, she held on to her mommy's arm. His large body shadowed the dim doorway and Samantha thought he looked like the mean giant in her picture book.

"Are you in here, bitch?"

Samantha felt her mother start to shake.

"Please. Samantha's in here with me."

"I don't give a damn!"

Her mother threw back the cover and stood. "You're drunk."

"Damn right I am, and I'm fixin' to have me a little of you."

Lena turned toward her daughter. "Sammi, run. Get out of here, now."

She was so scared she couldn't move. Her daddy could be real mean. When he would hit her mommy she wanted to hide in the closet to make it go away. Hugging her teddy bear, she watched the giant lean toward her. He smelled like the stuff in the bottle he always drank from. Her momma called it whiskey.

"Yeah, run, before I decide to have a piece of you too."

Samantha heard rage in her mother's voice.

"You keep your filthy hands off her. I'll die before I let you touch her."

She watched her father's fisted blow land on Lena's face, and felt the bed's movement as she fell. "Momma!"

"Go, Sam, run."

Samantha jumped out of the bed, but for some reason her legs wouldn't carry her away. She stood in horror as her mother screamed and her father grunted and made loud demands. He drew his hand back again and again and slammed his fist into her mother's face and body.

The thunder outside didn't scare her as much as her daddy did when he acted like this. Flashes of lightning brightened the small room. She saw blood on her momma's face. Her chest had never pounded like this before. She was so scared. She had to do something, but what could a little girl do.

Her father's gun was in the table drawer next to the bed. She knew because when he showed her how to use it, her mother became angry with him. Her mommy had said it was dangerous and told her never to touch it, but now she had to.

She willed her legs to run. Opening the drawer, she reached in. When she felt it she shivered. It was cold and heavy, but she lifted it. She had to help her mommy.

Holding it tight, she pointed it at her daddy. "Stop. Stop hurting my mommy!" She heard him laugh and, in a flash of lightning, saw that he was going to hit her momma again. "If you do that again, I'll shoot you! I promise, I will."

When the lightning lit the room once more, her daddy looked like the devil himself. His lips were curved in a scary smile and she thought he was really a monster. Then he hit her mommy again, but this time Mommy didn't move.

Samantha closed her eyes and squeezed the trigger. The loudest crack of thunder she'd ever heard rang in her ears. Her arms flew into the air, and she couldn't hold on to the gun, it went crashing to the floor behind her. She coughed from the nasty smell of smoke in the air and began to cry as she heard her father's body hit the ground on the other side of the bed.

Now it was quiet in her mommy's room. No screaming or yelling. Even the rainstorm outside wasn't noisy anymore.

"Mommy, Mommy." She ran to her, but she wouldn't get up.

The teddy bear lay at Samantha's feet. She picked it up and hugged it so she wouldn't be alone in the dark.

CHAPTER 3

A gentle shake to her shoulder brought Samantha out of her memory. "Oh, Momma, I killed my daddy."

"There, there, honey, it's over. That was twenty years ago." She cupped Samantha's face in her hands and gazed into her eyes. "You saved my life, Sammi. If you hadn't shot him, I would have died that night. He'd beat me before, but not like that."

"But what if I kill someone else?"

A smile crossed Lena's face. "You're not a killer. You were a frightened little girl and fate forced your hand."

Samantha fought the inner turmoil that verified she could never be close to a man for fear her temper would flare and she would kill him as she did her father. Her mind flashed back to Luke. She wanted him desperately, but couldn't allow it.

Months ago, when she'd met him, she thought it might be feasible. Today, her physical outburst when she slapped him, along with the onslaught of the nightmare, confirmed the impossibility.

Luke ran his fingers through his tousled hair. His attempt to sleep proved futile, so he pulled on his jeans and went outside.

He inhaled deeply. The scent of sage on the cool night air filled his lungs. He walked the length of the large wooden deck built around the perimeter of the house and sat on a wicker chair. The full moon loomed brightly in the Nevada sky, and crickets chirped their night songs.

Samantha's question rolled over and over in his mind. *What are you doing here? What are you doing here? What are you do—* What *was* he doing? Not only in her room but on this ranch? Did he actually want the responsibility of running a huge operation like this? He loved rodeo life. It was all he really knew.

He'd never been responsible for anything but his pickup and his horse. It wasn't a question of, could he do it? He knew he was capable of managing the affairs of the H-H. It was a question of, did he want to? And the appearance of Rain Storm complicated things even more. "I'm so confused."

An owl hooted from a nearby tree, and he chuckled under his breath. "Well, bird of wisdom, what do you suggest I do? Should I go back to the rodeo circuit where I belong? Or should I stay here and become a wealthy rancher? And what about Miss Storm? I guess I should get used to calling her Samantha Rainwater before I do anything else."

Hoot. Hoot.

"I knew you'd agree." Luke peered into the sky. Shadows covered the lunar surface. "How about you, man in the moon? What would you do?"

"Talkin' to someone?"

Luke turned toward the man's voice. "Johnny."

"I was just gonna turn in and thought I'd come out and have a smoke. Want one?" He thrust the pack in Luke's direction.

"No, thanks. Don't smoke."

"Good. It'll kill ya. Who was ya talkin' to?"

Luke watched the match head flare. Johnny had never been cordial before, but Luke welcomed the company even if he wasn't fond of his uncle. "The man in the moon."

"He cain't help ya."

He met Johnny's gaze. "Help me with what?"

"That hell cat in there. If I were you, I'd steer clear of her. She's a mean one."

Luke had disliked Johnny since the first day he arrived. His statement about Samantha didn't make it any better. He stood and walked to the door. "Thanks for the advice. I'm going to call it a night."

"Suit yourself, but she's dangerous."

Luke opened the screen and went into the house. He lay in the darkness of his room, knowing Samantha was just down the hall. He longed to go to her bed. His time with her in Vegas drifted across his memory. She was a wonderful woman. It made him wonder what Johnny meant by dangerous.

The chirping of birds floated through the open window on the morning breeze. Samantha watched the curtains ruffle, her mind focused on Luke's presence in the house. She knew she would have to face him sooner or later.

"Now is as good a time as any." She threw back the cover and inhaled a calming breath. Why did just thinking about him make her giddy inside? If only she could push the memories of making love with him to the back of her mind, but that was all but impossible.

She dressed. In cut off denim shorts and a light weight summer blouse, she left the security of her room and headed for the kitchen. The aroma of breakfast being cooked teased her stomach.

She approached her mother. "Good morning. Smells

wonderful, I'm starving." She picked up a piece of bacon and popped it into her mouth.

Lena made an attempt to smack her hand. "Stop that, young lady. You can wait and eat with the rest of us."

Sammi leaned against the counter. "Anything you want me to do?"

"You're asking if you can help? What's this world coming to?"

She wrinkled her nose. "Very funny, Momma. How's Howard this morning."

"Surprisingly, better." Lena smiled. "He's well rested and grumbling for his breakfast. Which is just about ready."

Samantha watched her mother carefully place portions of food onto a plate that set alongside orange juice and coffee on a bed tray. "I'll take it, if you don't mind."

"Be my guest." Lena handed the tray to Samantha. "I don't necessarily want to see the old grouch again this morning."

"Oh, Momma, you like Howard and you know it."

Lena gave her a warning glance. "Scoot."

Samantha made her way into Howard's room, amazed to see him sitting up in bed, his color close to normal. "Morning, Howie."

"And a beautiful morning it is, Sam."

She set the tray over his lap. "Breakfast is served." Howard's eyes seemed to sparkle when he looked at the food.

"I'm so hungry I could eat a bear."

Samantha's sorrows over the old man's illness began to lighten. "You're much better this morning."

"Damn right I am. Give me a few days and I'll be raring to go."

She was happy for his positive attitude. "You know, I think you will. If you keep eating like this, it may be tomorrow."

He took another bite. "Pull up a chair, Sam."

She did as instructed.

"Another nightmare last night?"

Samantha nodded. Would that night so many years ago ever stop haunting her?

"When he heard you scream, Luke ran out of here like a bat out of hell. I think he likes you."

She remembered the scene in her bedroom the night before. His gray eyes were riddled with concern, his touch gentle and caring and his voice reassuring. No, she couldn't allow herself to read something that wasn't there into his reaction. "I don't think so."

"Do you like him?"

She turned to face Howard. "Hey, what is this? Twenty questions?"

Howard sipped his juice then set the glass down. "Tell me about you and Luke."

She felt the color rush from her face. "There's nothing to tell." He eyed her questioningly.

"That's not what I hear."

"Who have you been talking to?"

"I have my sources."

"Well, your *source* has to be your son. He's the only one who knows anything."

"How'd he break your heart?"

She turned away once again hoping he wouldn't see the hurt in her eyes. "Break my heart? I don't know what he's told you, but if he said that, it's a lie."

"Come on, Sam, tell me about it."

She walked to the window and stared out. "Apparently you know everything all ready. You tell *me* what lies he told you."

"Well, here he is. Why don't you ask him yourself?"

She whirled around. Luke stood tall and so handsome it took her breath away. He could wear a pair of Wranglers better than any man she knew.

His silver-belly hat resting in his hands, brought back memories of the first time she saw him holding it just the same way. Her heart sank to the pit of her stomach as she tried to dismiss the recollection. Damn-it, why did the man make her feel this way?

Hoping he saw contempt in her eyes, she glared at Luke. "I wouldn't ask him spit." She had to get away from him for fear she'd make a fool of herself. She scurried past him and out the door.

Luke watched Samantha's backside as she walked down the hall. Her beauty floored him. He addressed his father. "What was that all about?" That was a dumb question. He knew what was wrong. Soon he'd tell her his reasons for leaving her in Vegas.

"Hell, boy, I don't know. What man can say what causes a woman to do anything?"

Luke scowled. "Did you say something to her about our little talk last night?"

"Mmm, not really; but we don't have time to discuss it now. You need to be getting into town. That lawyer's not going to wait forever."

"Dad, I'm not sure I'm ready for this. You seem much better today, maybe we should put the inheritance off for a while."

"I'm better today, but I could go to meet the Lord tomorrow. We can't put it off."

Guilt plagued Luke's heart. "Yes, but..."

"No buts. Let me tell you something. I worked all my life to build this ranch into what it is today. My dream was to have you take it over when I got too old. When your mother contacted me and said she thought it was time you and I got to know each other, I knew my dream had come true.

"I want you to have this ranch, son. As I've told you, the only stipulation is that Lena be cared for the rest of her life. That woman's been awfully good to me over the years, and I want her future to be secure."

"I understand." Lena was a wonderful woman. He already had a special spot for her in his heart, but was it really his place to do what his father requested?

"Good."

"Johnny's going to continue to foreman the hands, right?"

"What's wrong with you, boy? Why are you getting cold feet?"

"This is a sudden change for me."

"So is death for me. I could go any minute and this business wouldn't be taken care of. If you don't want to take over the ranch right now, you don't have to. You can get someone to do it for you. But you do have to sign those papers before it's too late."

"Do you think Johnny will cause trouble when he finds out you're giving the ranch to me?"

"Oh, he'll rant and rave, that's for sure. But he won't cause any problems. He doesn't know it yet, but I've given him a beautiful chunk of land in the west corner of the ranch, a wad of money too." Howard glanced at the clock on the nightstand. "You better get out of here now. You don't want to be late."

"Yes, sir." Luke walked toward the door then turned to face Howard. He realized he'd be a fool to give this up just because he wasn't sure he was ready to deal with it. "Thanks, Dad."

Samantha watched her mother approach the corral. For a woman in her late fifties, she was beautiful. "You look pretty today, Lena Rainwater. Are you going somewhere?"

"Yes, I have a date with a handsome man."

She knew Howard wasn't up to driving and wondered if one of the hands was going to take her into town. "Oh, really. And who might that be?"

"One, Luke Dilashaw."

Samantha consciously had to close her gaping mouth. "Luke?"

Lena laughed. "Yes. He's going to drop me at the grocery store while he takes care of some business in Elko. Want to come along?"

"Certainly not." The last thing she needed was to be stuck in the cab of Luke's pickup, smelling his musky scent and feeling the heat of his body so close.

"There's something between you two. I'm not blind."

"Don't you start too, Momma. I've heard enough from Howard this morning. I want you to know, as soon as he's up and around, I'm leaving. I have to get back to work."

"Don't you mean you have to get away from, Luke?"

Movement caught Samantha's attention. She turned. Luke walked across the lawn. His broad shoulders radiated confidence as he approached and her lungs refused to take in air when he glanced in her direction. Glad he didn't focus his attention on her, she allowed herself to breathe. Maybe if he ignored her, she could get through the next few days.

He met Lena's gaze. "Are you ready, Mrs. Rainwater?"

"Yes, I am."

Luke invited her to take his arm. "Shall we then?"

Samantha watched the attractive man of her dreams, and her mother, get into his four-by-four pickup and drive away.

CHAPTER 4

L uke glanced in his rear-view mirror at Samantha's tall, slim image. His loins tightened, and he shifted in his seat. He heard a slight giggle from the passenger side of the truck and turned toward Lena who studied him with a knowing smile and a sparkle in her eyes.

"She's beautiful, isn't she?"

He turned his gaze to the road. Flush heated his brow. "Yes, ma'am, she is." He recognized pride in her voice.

"Have you ever heard her sing?"

"Yes, ma'am."

"Good, isn't she?"

"She's great, Mrs. Rainwater."

"So, what's going on between you two?"

He glanced in her direction. "Have you been talking to my father?"

"Of course not. Why?"

"You two sound like a broken record."

"It's obvious you have feelings for each other."

He glanced back to the road. "Before I came to meet Howard, I went to Vegas to get my thoughts together. That's when I got to know Rain." Meeting Lena's questioning gaze he said, "Yes, I had strong feelings for her, but I didn't know what turns my life was about to take.

"After Mother told me that Joe Dilashaw wasn't my real father, I was angry at the world. Even at my age, finding out your birth father is someone other than you thought, can be hard to take. At that time I had no desire to meet Howard Hale, Then when I found out he was ill, I knew I couldn't put it off any longer. I didn't want my life to be left with questions and no answers. Rain got caught in between."

"Why did your parents keep Howard from you?"

"Mother knows I'm a lot like him. She was afraid I'd run away and come to live with him."

"I see."

"Lena, I wasn't sure what was going to happen when I left Vegas. The rodeo circuit was all I'd ever known, and Lord help us that's no life for a woman. I didn't know what kind of person Howard would be or what hardships these changes might bring. I couldn't subject Sammi to what could have been a roller coaster ride to hell."

"Those feelings for her are still there, Luke. You demonstrated them last night after her nightmare." She smiled. "What are you going to do?"

"I'm not sure, Lena. I'm not sure."

Samantha went into the house to inform Howard she was going horseback riding. She'd ridden these hills hundreds of times and knew them like the back of her hand. Today she thought she'd saddle up, strap her flattop guitar to her back, and ride her horse Markie down to Idaloo's. It would be fun to see the old crowd and get Luke off her mind. Forgetting how that man made her feel would be like forgetting she had a heart, but she had to try. If for nothing else, for his protection from her.

She secured her guitar strap to her guitar, flipped it onto her back and mounted Markie. She'd found this the easiest way to take her guitar with her when she was riding.

When she rode up to the front of Idaloo's, she smiled. The rustic old tavern looked the same. She stopped Markie, dismounted, and tethered the mare to the new hitching post old Ben Wiley put up some years back after a drunk ran over the old one.

Samantha brought her guitar from her back to the front and took the strap over her head so she could carry the instrument while she went inside. She quietly set the instrument by the door and took a seat at the bar. "Bag of chips and an un-cola, please."

As quickly as age allowed, the bent old bartender whirled in her direction. He squinted as if to get a better glimpse of her.

"Sam? Sammi Rainwater, that you?"

"In the flesh, Mr. Wiley." Fast as his feeble legs would carry him, he wended his way around the end of the bar.

"Well good golly, come here and give me a hug."

Samantha leaped off the stool and ran to meet the old fellow's open arms. "How are you, Ben?" She gave him one last squeeze then returned to her seat.

Ben Wiley shuffled back behind the bar. "Better than some and worse than others I suppose, Sam."

Samantha met friendly greetings from all directions. The regular daytime crowd was mostly retired people who gathered to play dominos and socialize. She'd grown to love these old folks, but when dusk came around, the crowd would change and young people would filter in to drink beer, play pool and strut their stuff on the small dance floor.

The little tavern attracted many of the buckaroos that worked at surrounding ranches. Buckaroos. She'd always thought it funny that hired hands were called that throughout Nevada. However, these men were real cowboys. They would stay on the range many weeks at a time, but come into town on their days off.

Surprisingly, they never caused much trouble at Idaloo's. Everyone loved and respected Ben and Ida Wiley. Besides, they knew Ben kept a forty-five pistol behind the bar that he wouldn't hesitate to use if any young buck called his hand.

Pats on the back and handshakes over, Samantha settled in and opened her bag of chips. "Ben, where's Ida?"

"She'll be along directly. She's getting my nephew settled."

"Oh, is Aaron visiting?" She rolled her eyes. "Great."

"I know you two have never hit it off, but a lot of years have passed, things may have changed. I hope so anyway, he's coming here to live."

She saw the sad expression cross Ben's face. "What's wrong, Ben?"

"Nothing really. It's just time Mother and I retired, and I'm having a hard time accepting it. Beings we never had any children, Aaron's going to take over for us."

"I think it's wonderful. You two won't be tied to this place twenty-four hours a day. You need to travel, see the world."

"That's exactly what we intend to do as soon as we show Aaron the ropes."

Samantha heard the familiar creak of the back screen door as it opened.

Ben glanced through the kitchen. "Here they are now."

Samantha greeted Ida with a hug, and offered a handshake to Aaron.

"Well, Sammi, you've grown up," Aaron said.

Samantha battled the urge to recoil when his cold hand grasped hers. She met a blue stare that was more chilled than his skin. He scrutinized her from head to toe.

"You've turned into a looker. What are you doing tonight?"

Ida punched Aaron with her fist. "Mind your manners."

Samantha wanted to outright slug him, but she voiced her blow instead. "Whatever it is, it won't involve you, Aaron Wiley."

"Still feisty. Nice. We don't find too many like you where I come from."

She could tell he'd become citified. His hair was puffed on the top, reminding her of Elvis; he wore designer clothes, his nails were manicured and painted with clear polish. He certainly didn't fit into the small community of Lamoille, and never did in her estimation.

"Let's hear some singin', Sam," came a request from one of the regulars.

"Yeah, sing to us," pitched in another.

"It's been a long time, Sam," said a third.

"Okay, okay." Samantha smiled and retrieved her guitar. She sat on a stool, and the folks gathered around. "I'll sing one for Ben and Ida called, 'Home Sweet Home'."

Samantha shuddered when she noticed Aaron's frosty glare. She turned away and attempted to warm the hearts of her small audience.

Luke hesitated before he signed on the dotted line, then penned his name, *Lucas D. Dilashaw*, onto the last document. Unable to believe the changes the last six months had brought, he pushed the stack of papers toward Jeff Paine, the lawyer handling the transaction

"That's it, Mr. Dilashaw. The H-H ranch is all yours. Well, at least when the old man dies, it will be. From what I hear, sounds like it'll be real soon."

Luke glared at him. "I'd thank you to keep your thoughts to yourself, Mr. Paine."

"I thought you'd be excited about inheriting a five-thousand-acre ranch?"

"Not at the expense of my father's life."

Paine smirked. "You're sure attached to someone you've just met. Course, money does that to people."

Luke stood, reached across the desk, grabbed the man by the collar and with one hand jerked him to his feet. "Mr. Paine, I haven't liked you since the first day we met, and I don't like you now. Didn't you say I have power of attorney over my father's affairs?"

Paine nodded his head.

Pulling Paine closer, Luke narrowed his eyes at the greedy lawyer. "Then you're fired." He shoved the disgruntled man back onto his overstuffed chair and released him in one movement, then turned toward the door.

Paine tugged on his suit and straightened his tie. "We'll see about that."

"*We* just did." Luke stepped outside and slammed the door behind him. His fist tightened, and his breathing labored, he took a long pause to calm down. How could a professional be so damned curt?

Outside, he glanced toward his truck. An advertising flyer had been placed under one of the windshield wipers. He calmed himself and looked at his watch, time to pick up Lena. Retrieving the paper from the window, he got into the truck then he laid it on the seat.

⚜

Luke steered the pickup truck around a corner. This wasn't right. The grocery store couldn't be down here. The street came to an abrupt end, and he pulled onto a graveled drive marked, private. He smiled when he read the hand painted sign on the front of the house. 'Norma's'. He'd almost forgotten brothels were legal in Nevada. This one apparently had good clientele. The sheriff's car was parked in the back.

He got back on the main road. When he pulled into the supermarket parking lot, Lena waited patiently outside. "Sorry I'm late. I took a wrong turn. You've got enough food here to feed a small army, Mrs. Rainwater." Luke loaded the heaping grocery bags into the back of his truck.

"With more than a dozen hands living in the bunk house at H-H, it takes a lot to satisfy their appetites. I'm just glad they have their own cook, and I don't have to do it anymore."

He helped her into the cab. "You used to cook for all of them?"

"There weren't so many back then. The ranch has steadily grown. Howard has hired more men than I can count over the last few years."

He shut her door and went around to the driver's side. When he started the engine, he noticed Lena reading the paper he'd tossed on the seat.

"Oh, my God! What are you going to do?"

He watched the color drain from her face. "About what?"

She shoved the paper toward him. "This."

A frown creased his brow. "What is it?"

"You didn't read it?"

"No. Someone left it on the windshield and I assumed it was an advertisement." He pulled to the side of the road. "Let me see it."

Lena wiped a tear and handed him the paper.

Luke read the pasted on, out of sorts lettering.

YOU ARE NOTHING BUT A GOLD DIGGER. WE KNOW YOU ARE TAKING ADVANTAGE OF OLD MAN HALE. GET OUT OF TOWN WHILE YOU STILL CAN. WE DON'T NEED YOUR KIND AROUND HERE, AND TAKE THAT NO GOOD INDIAN GIRL WITH YOU BEFORE YOU FIND HER DEAD IN A DITCH.

His heart hammered as he studied the threatening note. "Who the hell would do this? Do you have any ideas?" He glanced at the pained expression on Lena's face as she shook her head and he shared her anger. "Don't worry, ma'am, I won't let anything happen to Sammi." He scooted toward the older woman and embraced her.

She sobbed. "Why would anyone want to hurt my baby girl? She's loved by everyone who knows her."

"Calm down, Lena. We'll find who did this and put a stop to it. I promise."

Tears streamed down her cheeks. "You have to go to the police."

He released her, picked up his cell phone then put it back down. This was something he'd talk directly to his dad about. He put the pickup in gear and re-entered the flow of traffic. "Not just yet. I want to discuss this with my father first." The image of the sheriff's car at the brothel popped into his mind.

Samantha said her good-byes to the folks at Idaloo's, flipped her guitar to her back and left the building. She began checking to make sure her saddle was secured properly when jumped at the sound of a man's voice.

"Leaving so soon?"

She pivoted to see Aaron Wiley. Just as quickly, she turned back around and continued with what she was doing. "You shouldn't sneak up on people like that."

"Mmm, mmm, mmm. Nice butt."

Samantha twisted her neck around. Aaron Wiley's gaze was focused on her bottom. She twirled to face him. "Aaron, I don't know who you think you are, but I will not stand for this treatment. I would appreciate it if, in the future, you keep your distance."

"Oh, come on. I know what you've made of yourself,

Miss Hoity-Toity. A casino singer. Don't tell me you don't like it when a man wants to jump your bones."

Why did men think she was a plaything just because she was an entertainer? She closed her eyes, took a deep breath and forced her temper down. "I'll say this one more time." She met his gaze and clenched her teeth. "Stay away from me. You know what I'm capable of."

She turned toward Markie, put her foot in the stirrup, and hoisted herself into the saddle and made sure her guitar strap stayed securely in place. "Come on, Markie, let's get away from this creep."

The mare seemed more than happy to comply and broke into a cantor, kicking dust in Aaron's face. Samantha glanced over her shoulder in time to see him stumble. She stifled a laugh when his backside hit the ground.

CHAPTER 5

After unloading the groceries, Luke took the threatening letter to his father's room. He was delighted to see Howard sitting on a chair next to the bed. "Before you know it, you'll be trying to break another horse."

Howard's eyes glistened. "Son, have a seat. How was your day in town?"

He pulled up a chair. "Not real great, I'm afraid. I fired the lawyer."

"Haw, haw, haw. I've been wanting to do that for years just never got around to it. Did you smash his face in too?"

Whisking his fingers across his mustache, the corners of Luke's mouth lifted. "Came close."

Howard pounded the arm of his chair with his fist. "Damn," he said with disappointment.

"You're ornery."

"Just like my son, I expect. But I would have popped the SOB in the mouth."

Luke laughed. "If he wasn't a lawyer, I would have. But the jerk would win a lawsuit against me, and I couldn't stand to give him a dime."

"Go back and slug him andI'll bail you out."

He was sure the older man would do just that. "It's a

hell of a thought." He watched Howard laugh and was glad the old man was recovering. "See the doctor today?"

"Yeah, he said it's a miracle. He thought I'd be gone by now." Howard peered into Luke's eyes. "You and Sam have given me the will to live. I have to stick around to see what happens between you two."

The mention of Samantha brought the reason for his visit into focus. "Dad, if you feel up to it, I have something to show you. I warn you, it's not pleasant."

"I'm used to unpleasantries, boy. Hand it over."

Luke gave the papered message to Howard and watched as the old man's brow rumpled with concern.

"Hmm. Where'd this come from?"

"I found it on the windshield of my pickup truck."

"Does Lena know about it?"

"Unfortunately, she was the first one to read it."

"Who the hell would have a reason to do something like this? Did Lena have any ideas?

"No, she didn't. Do you think Johnny might have something to do with it? He and I talked last night. He doesn't like Samantha much, and he's not real fond of me."

"Don't like her. Well, why the hell not?"

"He didn't say."

"No, son, I don't think he did this, but we should investigate every possibility. I'll have a talk with him. In the meantime, you call Sheriff Johns, and ask him to come out here."

Luke thought of the patrol car and the bordello. "Does the sheriff have a habit of visiting the houses? I saw his car parked at Norma's earlier."

"Probably checking to make sure they're keeping everything legal. It's part of his job."

His father was right. "I'll give him a call."

From atop the north ridge, the sunset cast an eerie glow across the Nevada hills. It was one of Sammi's favorite sights. On her way home, she stopped Markie a short distance from the ranch house. "Isn't it beautiful, girl?" She patted the horse on the neck. "Too bad Luke Dilashaw isn't a nicer guy. If he didn't rile me so, it would be fun to have him to share this beauty with." She inhaled. "Take a deep breath, girl. Clean, fresh air, I love it here."

The sound of a car coming up the road gained her attention. In the dim light of dusk, she saw a reflection cast off the light bar atop the car. "The sheriff?" She watched as the vehicle pulled down the lane leading to house.

She feared something had happened to Howard. Her heart skipped a beat. "Let's go, Markie." .

⨎ ⨍

"Coker Johns, this is my son, Luke Dilashaw."

"Nice to meet you. Damn, you got eyes like your daddy."

Luke smiled and accepted the young sheriff's handshake. "I'll take that as a compliment."

Howard spoke from his bed. "Luke's taken over my legal matters, Coke. We'll discuss things, but he's the one who will make the final decisions."

"Looks like you've stepped in something here, Luke."

He glanced at the bottom of his boot. "Yeah, and I'm not sure what it is."

Chuckles filled the room then Luke took the floor. "Sheriff Johns—"

"Please, call me Coke."

"Alright, Coke. I ran across a slight problem while I was in town today." Luke handed Coker the paper. "This was left on my windshield."

Luke's attention was drawn away from the sheriff when the door swung open.

Samantha put her guitar down, ran across the room and embraced Howard. "Are you okay?"

"Of course, I am. Why?"

"I saw the sheriff's car and thought something was wrong."

"I'm fine." Howard gestured toward the sheriff. "You remember Coke, don't you?"

Luke watched Samantha's gaze meet Coke's and thought he saw a spark ignite between them.

Samantha approached Johns with open arms. "Coke, it's good to see you. It's been a long time."

Coke's arms surrounded Samantha's waist and pulled her close. "Too long, Sam."

Jealousy surfaced in Luke when Samantha seemed to enjoy the embrace. The second man today he felt like punching.

Battling the craving to rush across the room and rip the two apart, he inhaled deeply and waited for the scene to end. Johns' hands cupped Samantha's face. Their gazes locked. Was Johns going to try to kiss her? The bastard! Luke stepped forward and grabbed Samantha's shoulder.

"Excuse me, but we have business to tend to here." He gestured toward the door. "If you don't mind."

Samantha yanked free of his grasp. "I beg your pardon." She shifted her gaze toward Coke. "I apologize for Mr. Dilashaw's rudeness. Will I see you later?"

He smiled and nodded his head. "When we're through here."

Samantha turned and glared at Luke. "I'll be on the back deck, *Coker*."

Luke watched Sam stomp out, chin high and shoulders straight, she slammed the door. He shouldn't have reacted like a jealous kid, but when his dad wrinkled his nose, he couldn't help it. For a father he'd just met, Howard read him like a book. The amused look on Howard's face told him the old codger was enjoying the fireworks.

Luke gritted his teeth and fought the slight tremor in his hand when he swiped his finger across his mustache. He glanced toward Howard. The old man's lips were raised at the corners. "Something funny?"

"No, no, not at all."

Clearing his throat, Luke looked at Johns. "Let's get back to business." He wanted to wipe the smirk off Coke's face.

"Yes." Coke studied the page of disjointed letters. "It looks like this might be serious."

Luke's voice carried authority. "I think Samantha should remain on the ranch until this thing's cleared up."

"Well, I wouldn't go tha—"

"You might not, Sheriff Johns, but I would. She's not to leave the property until we find out who is responsible for this and proper action is taken. She's safer here than off somewhere by herself." Luke shifted his gaze. "Dad?"

Howard nodded.

Coker stepped toward the bed. "Howard, don't you think that's going too far? After all, she has a career to think of, and this could be nothing more than a joke."

"Coke, I told you, Luke's making the decisions around here now. I won't go against him."

The sheriff shook his head. "Well, she's not going to like it."

"Like it or not, that's the way it's going to be." Luke walked to the bedroom door and opened it, inviting the sheriff to leave. "I'll call if we need you, Johns. If you hear anything let me know. You'll have to call the landline, no cell reception out here."

Luke found himself easily slipping into his new role. Or was it his drive to keep Samantha safe that compelled his actions?

"He what?" Samantha's voice rang through the hills. She stood and paced the wooden deck. "Who does he think he is?"

Coker sat down. "Calm down, Sam, it's for your own good."

The crisp night air did little to cool her temper. "Luke Dilashaw has no say over what I do." She glanced up hearing the thump of boot heels against the hardwood floor in the hallway. "What would even give him the idea to imprison me in my own home?" Luke's broad shoulders filled the doorway, blocking out the light from within the house.

He stepped outside, approached Samantha and handed her a piece of paper. "This."

Coker Johns rose to his feet. "I'd better be going."

Samantha laid the page aside. "Okay, Coke. I think Luke and I have a few things to discuss."

"I'll call you tomorrow, Sam."

"Do that." She defiantly shifted her gaze to Luke. "I'll come into town and see you."

As Coke's shadow faded into the darkness, Luke spoke softly. "Read that, please."

She picked it up. The porch light illuminated the deck, allowing her to read the lettering. A lump formed in her throat as she followed the words. She swallowed hard to push it back into its proper place. "Someone's threatening my life?"

"It looks that way."

"Does my mother know about this?"

"Yes."

"She must be worried sick. I'd better go talk to her."

Luke gently grabbed her arm as she passed. "Lena agrees with me."

"About what?"

"You staying on the property."

"You've talked to her about it already?"

"Howard, too."

"This is a conspiracy." She wrenched her arm away from his grasp. Entering the house, she wondered why her skin seared with his every touch.

Why was Luke acting so protective? And his jealous outbreak with Coke had been downright, embarrassing. He was assuming way too much where she was concerned and she intended to put a stop to it.

Hoot. Hoot.

Luke glanced toward the friendly sound of the owl. "You're back, you old hooter. Good, I need someone to talk to.

"My life has taken so many turns over the last few months. I've gotten to know my real father, inherited a ranch, met the woman of my dreams, and she's driving me crazy."

He leaned back in the chair. "She's all I think about. Every time I see her, I want to hold her. Now her safety's at stake and it's up to me to watch after her."

Tilting his face to the heavens he swore. "I'll protect her with my life."

CHAPTER 6

Samantha eased through the doorway of Howard's bedroom. The morning sun silhouetted his broad shoulders and tall frame as he stood by the window "Here's your breakfast."

He turned to face her. "Thanks, Sam."

Why hadn't she noticed Luke's resemblance to Howard the first time she saw him? It was uncanny how much the two men were alike only to have known each other for six months.

Howard walked toward her. "What's wrong? You look like you've seen a ghost."

She closed her gaping mouth. *A ghost indeed.* "I'm just surprised to see you up and walking." She set the tray on the bedside table and helped him to a chair. "What happened to your heart monitor?"

"Doc said my heartbeat's been steady the last few days. He sees no need to keep me on that blasted thing. I'm getting my strength back, too."

She laughed when Howard flexed his biceps. "I'm glad to hear that, because you need it to do all the griping you do. By the way, when are you planning to take the ranch affairs over again?"

He picked up his coffee cup. "I'm not."

Her stomach did flip flops. "You're not? Howard are you crazy? You've barely known Luke Dilashaw six months, and you're willing to hand him everything you've worked for?"

"Sam, listen I—"

"No, you listen. You're going to live a hundred more years, and I'm going to do all I can to stop you from giving up your life's work."

Howard groaned. "Don't forget who you're talking to, young lady. I may be sick, but I'm not dead."

"I don't mean to be disrespectful." She couldn't stand the thought of him losing everything he owned, especially to someone who was practically a stranger.

She sat in the chair across from him. Closing her eyes, she tilted her head back and took a deep breath. "I'm sorry, Howie. I'm just concerned. Are you sure you can trust Luke?" She didn't trust him.

"Are your mother and I the only ones that has faith in Luke? I had an extensive investigation completed on him and his stepfather. Neither one of them have done a rotten thing in their lives."

She couldn't say it out loud, but it went through her mind. *Except for breaking my heart.*

"Joe Dilashaw was a fine respectable man, and he raised my son in the same fashion." Howard peered into the air. "I'll always be grateful to the man for that."

"Yes, but Howard, what if there's something hidden in his past your investigator didn't find."

He smiled, reached across and patted her face. "There's not, Sammi. There's not."

She forced a grin. "Probably not." She didn't know why she suspected Luke. Just because he'd shattered on her heart, didn't mean he'd do the same to his father's. She rose, ambled behind the old man and placed her arms around his chest. "I'm glad you're better, Howie. I'll be a good girl, I promise." She kissed his cheek.

He continued with his breakfast. "I'll believe that when you mind Luke's rules and stay on the property."

She dropped her arms and huffed. "Surely you don't expect me to do that. Do you?"

"Yep."

Samantha twisted around. "Damn!" She turned and walked out. Luke had come into her life and turned it upside-down. She wished she could say she hated him; but on the contrary, she thought she loved him and it infuriated her.

Lena wiped her hands on her apron. Samantha stormed past the kitchen door. "What now?" Lena walked to Howard's room.

Howard glanced up when Lena entered. "It sure is good to have some life in the house again. I love your daughter's spunk."

"What's she being spunky about this time?"

"She doesn't like the fact that I have already handed everything over to Luke. Says I can't trust him. I think she's the one who can't trust him."

Lena nodded. "You've noticed the sparks between them, too?"

"More like flames."

She took a seat. "What are we going to do? We can't let this escalate into something dangerous."

"Now, Lena. Don't you be thinking about what happened to you twenty some years ago. This is nothing like that. They're in love, not hate. They'll work it out between themselves. If they don't, we might have to help them along." He met her gaze. "Without their knowledge, of course." He grinned.

Samantha sat on one of the Adirondack chairs in the yard. She'd come to terms with having to stay at the ranch until they got this mess cleared up, but she had a hard time accepting the fact that Luke would always be so close. Too close.

His presence made it hard for her to think. She longed to be in his arms. Kiss his lips. Have his tongue perform magical wonders across her skin. Her gaze drifted over the far away hills. "Luke Dilashaw, why do you do this to me?"

She rose and went into the house. In her room she changed her clothes from shorts and tennis shoes, to jeans and boots.

Making her way down the hall, she searched every room for her mother, and found her in Howard's bedroom. "What are you two conspiring against me now?" she asked.

Lena rose from her chair. "Honey, you have to comply with Luke's wishes. He knows what's best."

For a moment, Sammi's temper soared. How could he know what was best for her? She mentally counted to ten. "Don't worry, Momma, I'll stay on the ranch until, well, until I have to go back to work. Luke has two weeks to solve this puzzle, then I'm gone."

Samantha glanced up to see the pleased expression on Howard's face as she accepted her mother's embrace. She pushed Lena to arm's length and looked into her eyes. "I'm going riding. I won't go far so don't worry. Okay?"

Lena nodded and pulled a tissue from her apron pocket. She sniffed and wiped away a tear. "Thank you, baby girl."

Samantha released her mother's arms. "For what? Agreeing to stick around and bug you and Howard another two weeks?" A mischievous grin marked her face. "I'm going to make life miserable around here."

She turned and as she walked down the hallway, the

thought of actually leaving the ranch tore at her. Life on the road was lonesome. Here people and things she cherished surrounded her.

She loved her music too, but it didn't compare to the feeling of freedom she had when she rode Markie through the hills of the H-H, or the warmth and devotion in the house on special occasions, her mother being close enough to hug. These were the things she missed when she was gone, but how else could she make her living?

Luke decided to pay a visit to the sheriff's office, and he didn't like the turn the conversation had taken.

"I haven't heard anything."

"I don't believe you, Johns. Tell me."

Coke calmly sat in the chair behind his desk. "Mr. Dilashaw, I don't have to tell you jack."

Luke's head began to throb. Everywhere he'd turned today had resulted in a dead end. He wasn't about to let it happen again. He sat opposite the sheriff. "We're talking about Sammi's life. I thought you were her friend."

"What's that supposed to mean?"

Fighting to keep his composure, Luke took off his hat and placed it in his lap. "It means, if you're such good friends, you'd want to take every precaution to keep her out of danger. Including confiding in others so they might offer their help. That's all I'm doing Johns, offering help."

"It seems to me you're trying to take over."

If you only knew how deeply my feelings for her go, you'd understand. "No, not take over, just get people on the ball. I don't believe in waiting for things to happen, I believe in making them happen." He witnessed the look in Coker's eyes soften.

"Alright, Dilashaw, you win. Someone at the hardware store next door to Jeff Paine's office saw the man who put the paper on your window that day."

The muscles in his jaw tightened. Maybe this was the clue they needed. "Who was he?"

"We don't know. He was a buckaroo."

"Well, hell, there are hundreds of buckaroos around here. It could be anyone."

"Apparently this man walked with a distinct limp in his right leg. Know anyone like that?"

Luke could have kicked himself for not paying more attention to the men employed at the H-H, but why would one of them want him out of the picture or threaten Sammi's life? He racked his brain to remember anyone that fit that description. "No."

"You keep an eye out. We'll keep asking questions. If I hear any news, I'll let you know."

"Thanks." For a moment, Luke considered swallowing his pride and asking Coke Johns what he and Sammi's relationship was. *It's none of your business Dilashaw.*

He needed to hold his growing feelings for her inside. She obviously didn't like him, and he'd be damned if he tried to force himself into her life any more than necessary. He stood and shook Coke's hand.

Samantha hoisted the saddle onto Markie's back. "This is a good day for a ride in the hills. That's 'staying on the property' even if I'm not around the house. Right, girl? Maybe Luke won't horse whip me for that." She glanced up and patted the mare on the neck. "No offense."

After securing the saddle, she mounted. She was completely at ease on Markie. Howard had given the colt to her for her twenty-first birthday. It was hard to believe almost five years had passed since that day. Every time she came home, she spent time riding. She clicked her tongue and heeled Markie's sides. "Let's go."

Peeking through the curtain of the bunkhouse, Johnny Hale spoke to his side kick. "There she goes, Frank. I knew it wouldn't be long before she took a ride." He turned toward the lanky middle-aged man. "We're gonna follow her. See where she's goin'. Make sure she doesn't spot you though, she's a Nativewith eyes like an eagle."

Frank nodded his head. "What are we going to do when we find her?"

"Nothin' this time. She has a favorite place out there somewhere. I want to find out where it is. The next time she's out by herself, we'll know where she's going, and we'll be waiting for her. Then we can get down to business and put a little scare into her."

"Hey, Johnny, I appreciate you giving me a place to stay and all, but when I got out of prison, I swore I wouldn't get into trouble again."

"Don't wimp out on me, Frank. If we play our cards right, we can point the finger at that no-good nephew of mine." Johnny paced the hardwood floor of the bunkhouse. "If my brother thinks I've been slavin' around here for years just to be left out in the cold, he's got another think comin'. No, I intend to get my share of this place, legal or not."

"What about me?"

"Don't you worry. You scratch my back, I'll scratch yours. We were cell mates, now we're partners."

Frank stood. "Let's do it."

CHAPTER 7

L uke thought of Samantha all the way back from Elko. He passed through the tiny town of Lamoille and glancing over at Idaloo's, was glad Sammi's red Mustang wasn't in the dirt parking lot.

He drove up the lane of the H-H, awed by the overwhelming beauty of the log home atop the hill. If he decided to stay, it would become his home.

When he entered the ranch house, aromas of fresh baked pies met him at the door. His mouth watered as he walked into the kitchen.

Lena pulled a pie out of the oven. She placed it on a rack and glanced in his direction. "Hi."

"Hi, Lena. Smells wonderful. Are we having a party?" He viewed a dozen pies cooling.

"No, just making a treat for the hands. They've been working hard breaking all those new horses. I've seen you out there on that big, black stallion. You've hit the dirt a couple of times."

"Yeah, and I'll probably hit it a few more. He's a tough one, but I'll get him."

"I'm sure you will. Now, if you'll hand me a couple of plates then go see your daddy, I'll serve you guys a dish of ice cream and hot pie."

Luke scurried to the cabinet, fetched the plates and set them on the counter. "Where is he?"

"Believe it or not, he's in his study. I'm amazed how quickly he's recovering. So is Doc Stone. I only hope it isn't temporary."

"Me too." He leaned over one of the steaming pies, closed his eyes and inhaled. "Mmm. Where's Sammi?"

"She's out riding her horse."

His pulse skipped a beat. "Alone?" Lena's reassuring smile somewhat eased his worry.

"She knows these hills like the back of her hand, and she promised she wouldn't go far. She'll be okay."

His concern remained. He would have to tell Samantha she couldn't ride without an escort. Luke eyed the pies again. "I'd better get in the study. We wouldn't want our pie to get cold before you bring it to us."

When Luke entered the room, Howard was sitting behind a large oak desk. He glanced up over half-rimmed reading glasses that rested mid-way down his nose and grinned showing straight, white teeth.

"You're walking tall and proud today. If I had a world championship bronc riding buckle like that one, I would be too."

World champion. Somehow those words seemed foreign to him. When he thought about being world champion, he found the rodeo life calling to him, but he pushed it out of his mind. He had to stay put. Samantha was now his main concern.

"Have a seat. Any news?"

Luke removed his silver-belly hat, laid it aside and sat opposite his father. "Someone saw the man who put the paper on my window. Said he walks with a limp. Do we employ anyone who limps?"

Howard shook his head. "Not to my knowledge."

"I'd like to meet all the hands personally. Find out about their backgrounds and how long they've worked for you."

"That can be arranged." Howard stood and walked to a sizable oak filing cabinet. "I haven't kept good records for the last couple of months, but I have information on the men that were hired before that."

"Great, I'll go through those files this evening."

"You guys ready for pie?"

Howard turned at the sound of Lena's voice. "Pie?"

"Your favorite. Apple."

"Are you trying to kill me? The doctor told me to watch my diet."

"Oh, stop fussing Howard. I've prepared you a special low-fat one."

His nose wrinkled. "Sounds scrumptious."

She set the tray, none too lightly, on top of his desk. "You'd gripe if you were hung with a new rope, Howard Hale. One of these days I'll do something to satisfy you, then *I'll* be the one to drop dead with a heart attack." She placed her hands on her hips and turned

Luke watched Lena stomp out of the room and saw the smile on Howard's face.

Howard met Luke's gaze. "See where Sam gets it?"

Luke took another bite and nodded. "They're a lot alike."

"Like father like son. Like mother like daughter."

Luke saw admiration in his father's eyes. He wondered why the two older people hadn't become a couple over the years. It was obvious they were attracted to each other.

Howard put some pie in his mouth. "Hey, this isn't too bad."

"Mine's awesome. Maybe you should go tell Lena you like it."

"Maybe."

Horse hooves beating against the ground, grabbed his attention. He heard hard footsteps on the back deck, then the slamming of the door.

"Luke! Luke!"

The alarm in Sammi's voice drew him to his feet. His pulse beat in his temple and he prayed she wasn't hurt. He rushed down the hall and when he saw her, he knew something had happened.

All color had drained from her face. He pulled her into his arms and felt the pounding of her heart. "What is it, sweetheart?"

Sammi melted into Luke's protective embrace. "Someone fired a gun. I took Markie out for a ride, and someone took a shot at me." Her heart hung heavy in her chest, and she wanted to hide in Luke's arms for a lifetime.

"How long ago?"

"Not more than ten minutes." His warmth quelled the chill she'd gotten when she heard the bullet whiz by her ear. "What are we going to do?" she muttered. He kissed her forehead before he gently released her.

"I'll call Johns."

Their gazes locked. The worry she read in his eyes caused her pulse to quicken and air to rush into her lungs. She wondered what his true feelings were at that moment. And later would he be furious with her for leaving the house? If he was, he had a right to be, she'd acted like an idiot.

She didn't want to admit it, but he'd been right about her restriction. His actions told her he'd protect her from danger, but who would protect her heart from him.

He glanced at Lena. "Take care of her."

Lena nodded. "Are you okay, honey?"

"Yes, Momma, just a little shaken." She watched Luke disappear into Howard's study. She longed to run after him and stay by his side where she felt safe. But she wasn't safe, and neither was he. They were danger to each other. He could break her heart again, and the horror that she might kill him, just as she had her father, filled her soul.

She had to control her emotions, but she hadn't counted on being shot at. Fear for her own safety had driven her into his arms. She hoped her concern for his safety would keep her from seeking his embrace again.

❧

Johnny was furious as he and Frank rode the back way to the ranch. "I didn't tell you to take a shot at her, Frank. Damn, what were you thinking?"

"I didn't take a shot at her."

"Then who did? We were the only ones out there besides her."

"Dang it, Johnny. Don't you get it? If I didn't shoot at her and you didn't either, we couldn't have been the only one's out there."

A smile lifted the corners of Johnny Hale's mouth. "You're right." He laughed. "Hell, Frank, someone else is takin' care of our problem for us."

"Does that mean we don't have to worry about scarin' em' off anymore?"

"I didn't say that. We'll keep a lookout. If Luke and Samantha ain't gone in a few days, we'll still have to do somethin' about it."

❧

Samantha lay on her bed and hugged her pillow. Her trembling had finally subsided. The sound of the gunshot that echoed through the hills earlier in the afternoon, now echoed in her mind. She closed her eyes and covered her ears as if that would block out the sound, but pictures of a stormy night twenty years ago flashed behind her lids.

She couldn't stay cooped up in this room any longer. Opening the door, she stepped into the hallway where the sound of Luke and Howard's voices came from the study.

She walked down the hall and entered the room. Her gaze immediately joined with Luke's. He held out his hand, inviting her to take it. She tried but couldn't stop herself from accepting the temptation. Their fingers clasped and tingles shot up her arm as he pulled her onto his lap.

"How are you?"

"Better." His show of affection momentarily dissolved any hope she had of distancing herself from him. The world around them seemed to disappear. His clean smell drifted into her nostrils, and she inhaled deeply.

Howard cleared his throat. "Sam, we're having a meeting here. If you'd like to join us, take a chair."

Samantha glanced over at Howard then at Coker Johns. "Coke, I'm sorry, I didn't see you."

He raised an eyebrow. "Yes, I noticed."

Heat rushed to her face in a flush. Why did Luke make her act like a fool every time she got near him? She quickly stood and took a seat in a vacant chair next to Coker. "Have you learned anything, Coker?"

"I had some officers up there earlier looking for clues, but it's getting too dark now. We'll go back up tomorrow and take another look around. Did it sound like a rifle or a handgun, Sam?"

The sound of the shot rang in her memory once again. "A rifle. Large caliber."

Luke swiped at his mustache. "Could you tell what direction it came from?"

"I couldn't, but Markie turned her head to the north when she heard it."

As he spoke, Howard ran his hands up and down the arms of the large leather chair behind his desk. "From the location y'all described, the road lies just north of that hill. Someone could have easily hiked up and waited for her to ride by."

Luke addressed his father. "Yes, but who would have known she'd be riding today?"

"Anybody who knows Sammi knows she rides every day. And lots of folks around here know her."

"Boy, that narrows it down," Coke said.

"Would you guys please stop talking about me like I'm not in the room? I might have some input here."

Luke turned toward her. "Like what, sweetheart?"

Sweetheart? It was the second time that day he'd called her that. What were his motives, why was he so concerned about her safety? For that matter, why did she care about his well-being? She knew darn good and well what her feelings were, but what were his?

Trying to get her mind on matters at hand, she forced herself to speak. "Yes, it was the ridge just south of the road. I ride up there all the time to watch the sunset. I think just about everyone that knows I ride a lot knows that. It only takes a short time to get up that hill on foot, and a lot less time to get down. Someone could easily park below and make the climb in no time. As a matter of fact...—"

Her blood ran cold. She remembered as a child she'd seen Aaron Wiley on that ridge many times. He'd glare at her when she'd ride by. "Someday I'm going to have a horse too, Miss Hoity-Toity," he'd yell. No, he was a creep, but he didn't have the guts to shoot at her.

"Sammi, what's wrong?"

She met Luke's gaze. "Noth—nothing . I remembered something."

"Anything that will help us with the case?" Coke asked.

"No." Her feelings for Aaron had never been of friendship, but Ben and Ida were important to her. Maybe after things settled down, she would confront Aaron herself.

CHAPTER 8

The full moon illuminated the sky, making leafy shadows waltz across the lawn. Luke strolled across the yard, pulled a long blade of grass, stuck the end in his mouth and leaned his shoulder against a tree.

Confusion burdened his thoughts. Sammi's emotions seemed to be on again off again, but so did his. Why had he invited her to sit on his lap? Was it to make Coker Johns jealous? Were his actions purely selfish? What was happening to him? He shook his head and spoke to the air. "Questions, questions."

He had to make a decision about his future. Each day he found himself missing life on the circuit less and less. Was it because this ranch would be his someday? Or was it Sammi's presence?

He was sure of one thing, he had to find out who was making the threats, then put a stop to it. He couldn't let anything happen to her. Even if he decided to go back on the road, Sammi would have to be safe before he did.

Crickets chirped, and in the distance, frogs called to their mates just as he wanted to call to Samantha. He'd never ached to hold a woman before he met her. "Damn what she does to me."

He studied the star-filled expanse above and the

Nevada hills silhouetted against the blue-black canvas of night. The green taste of the fresh grass blade journeyed to his senses. Who was out there that tried to hurt her?

Quiet footsteps interrupted his thoughts. He pushed himself off the tree and turned. His feelings surged as moonbeams filtered through the trees and captured the beauty of Samantha's amber eyes when she glanced at him.

"Luke, can we talk?"

"Sure."

"This is a stupid question, but..."

He smiled when she hesitated. "But, what?"

"Would you hold me for a minute?"

"That's not stupid, Sammi. We all need a hug now and then." He needed it too. Drawing her into his arms, he closed his eyes and inhaled the honeyed essence of vanilla from her hair. The smell of her, the feel of her against him caused his pulse to race. To savor her sweetness, he held his breath for a long measure. Silence was truly golden.

He stroked her hair and marveled how soft and silky it felt. She snuggled deeper into his embrace. Twisting gently from side to side, he rocked her. He should have denied her request. She had to be acting out of anxiety over the day's events, not from feelings for him. It wasn't fair to take advantage of her weak moment like this, but when it came to Sammi, he had no willpower.

He glanced down and met her gaze. Impulse conquered logic, and in the twinkling of a star, he kissed her. Molten desire surged through his body when her arms encircled his neck, and her tongue probed his mouth. He wanted her. More than anything he needed her, but he had to fight his yearning.

It took every ounce of his inner strength to leave her warmth, but when their lips parted he released his embrace. "Samantha, we can't." The pain he read in her eyes threatened to break his courage as she abruptly turned and walked away. "Wait, you don't understand. Let me explain."

She stopped and faced him. "You don't have to explain anything, Luke. I understand perfectly."

One of the hardest things he'd ever done was to leave her in Las Vegas, but that didn't hold a candle to his longing to go after her now. Would she ever believe he was only trying to protect her from his own confusion?

As Samantha walked away from Luke, a sinking feeling in her stomach forced bile into her mouth but finally it subsided. How could she have been such a fool? What was that old saying? 'Fool me once, shame on you. Fool me twice, shame on me.' She should have known better. Damn men anyway.

All she'd wished for was his company, and he'd assumed she wanted to make love. Well, he'd never have to speculate about her actions again. Horses would grow horns before she'd pursue consolation about anything from Luke Dilashaw.

She went into her room and readied for bed. No matter how hard she tried to stop it, Luke's kiss played repeatedly in her mind. Tracing her lips with her tongue she could still taste him. Why did life and love have to be so exhausting?

She laid her head on her pillow and was almost asleep when a clap of thunder sounded. Her eyes opened to the darkness and a sudden flash of lightning lit her room. Memories of the past drenched her mind as the rain fell outdoors. Fearing the onslaught of her nightmare, she fought sleep, but sometime in the early morning hours it prevailed.

When she awakened, she got up and went to the window. Pulling back the curtain, she saw the gray overcast sky that loomed above. She knew she had to face Luke one way or the other. The gloom of the clouds reflected the feeling in her heart perfectly.

After a shower, she drifted into the kitchen where her

mother sat reading a magazine. "Not cooking breakfast this morning?"

Lena glanced at her daughter. "No. The men went into town early. I thought you and I could have something light."

Sammi opened the cabinet and chose a dry cereal. "Looks like I'm stuck with frosted what-ever-they-are today." She took a banana from the fruit bowl and retrieved the milk from the fridge.

"Sleep good last night?"

The tone of Lena's voice caused Sammi to eye her suspiciously. "Yes. Why? "

"You had a hard day yesterday. And then the storm, I just wanted to make sure you didn't have a nightmare."

Sammi's mind went back to last night's encounter with Luke. "Not a nightmare, only a bad dream."

"Oh, honey, I'm sorry."

She set her filled bowl on the table. "No, Momma. It's nothing like it sounds," she said then began to eat.

"So, it wasn't the same as always?"

"No. Don't worry, I'm alright." For a few moments, Sam enjoyed the comfortable silence between her and Lena. Then she noticed her mother's questioning smile. "What?"

"Are you sure there's nothing you want to tell me?"

"Like what?"

"Anything about you and Luke?"

Her hunger fled with the mention of his name. "There's nothing to tell. He's a jerk."

"Sammi, you can't mean that. He's a fine young man, and he has eyes for you."

She stood and poured her half-eaten breakfast down the garbage disposal. "Oh, Momma, please." She recalled the way his gray eyes shined in the moonlight the night before.

"No, Sam, I can see it. Give it a chance. You'll see,

you two are made for each other."

"There's nothing between us; and there never will be."

"But..."

"I don't want to talk about Luke." She faced her mother, leaned against the counter and crossed her arms. "Let's talk about...Howard."

"*I* don't want to talk about Howard."

She met her mother's gaze and laughter filled the room.

Howard followed Luke into the sheriff's office. "It feels good to be out of the house."

"I hope you're not overdoing it by coming into town with me."

"I'm fine, boy. Don't worry."

They entered Coker Johns' private office, and Howard offered a handshake. "Coke, how are you?"

"Fine, sir. You're looking much better."

"I am better."

Luke took a seat next to his dad. "Have you heard anything?"

"Nothing. I sent two deputies back out to the sight this morning to look for evidence, but they haven't returned or called in. I'm expecting them to any time."

Howard cleared his throat. "What kind of evidence are we talking about here?"

"Spent cartridge, footprints, trash the suspect may have left behind."

A woman peered through the glass door then gave a slight knock.

Coker motioned her in.

"Sheriff, Deputy Roberts is on the radio. Do you want me to have dispatch route it in here?"

"Please."

Moments later static crackled through the small two-way radio. "Sheriff, you there?"

"Ten-four, Roberts. What did you find?"

"Nothing, sir. Looks like there could have been footprints, but whoever this was covered their tracks by brushing a dead limb over them. We found the branch we suspect they used, but fingerprints will be next to impossible to find on this thing."

"Bring it anyway."

"Ten-four."

Coke turned toward father and son. "Looks like we might have our first piece of evidence, men."

CHAPTER 9

Samantha bounded into the sewing room where Lena was mending some rag-tag jeans for one of the ranch hands. "Momma, I'm going to Idaloo's. There's someone there I want to talk to."

"Sammi, you can't go anywhere. Luke told you to stay on the property."

Pain returned to her heart with the reference to Luke. "I'll be back before he is, I promise. He'll never know I left unless you tell him."

"It's not just that. Someone shot at you yesterday."

"Believe me, I'm not forgetting." That's exactly why she wanted to talk to Aaron Wiley.

"Then why are you taking the chance?"

"Because I don't think I'm in any real danger, and I'm confident I can get to the bottom of this." The sooner she stopped Aaron from acting like an imbecile, the faster she'd be able to leave the ranch and get away from Luke.

Lena stood and hugged her daughter. "Please, baby girl, be careful."

Samantha returned her embrace. "I will, Momma, and I'll be back in a flash." She turned to leave, then faced her mother once again. "I love you, Lena Rainwater."

Wind whirled through the cab of the pickup. Luke glanced at his father. "What do you make of all this?"

Howard held another written warning in his hand. "I don't know how they're getting close to your truck without people seeing them."

"And who in their right mind would do it in front of the Elko County Sheriff's office? Read it to me again, Dad."

Howard placed his glasses on his nose and held the paper in front of him. *"This is your second warning, gold digger. Get out of town. Yesterday's miss will be tomorrow's hit. That half-breed isn't worth losing your life over. Take her and go."*

"I went through your employee files last night and didn't find anyone that seemed suspicious. Is there someone besides me and Johnny who might be entitled to inherit your fortune?"

"I have nobody else."

If it was the last thing he did, Luke was going to find the culprit that threatened him and Samantha. "There has to be a hidden clue somewhere. Something we're overlooking."

"Let's stop at the ridge and see if we can find anything."

"I don't think you need to be climbing hills in your condition. You need to get home and rest a while."

Howard bowed his head. "Yeah, I guess you're right. I can't believe Coker was already gone from his office when you took this back into the station. But emergencies come up quick. Oh well, it won't do us any good to fret about it now. When we get home, we'll call him."

Luke wondered why Johns had left the office in such a hurry. No one at the desk knew where he'd gone. The man was probably doing exactly what Howard had said, his job.

"Yeah, maybe by then he'll have found something." Why was he so doubtful of Coker Johns?

Howard laid the paper in the seat. "Changing the subject, let's stop at the feed store on the way out. We need to make an order. Say, how you coming on breaking that black stallion?"

Luke's head ached and he welcomed the new topic. "I haven't had a chance to climb on him for the last couple of days. Today would be a good day to try him again."

"How many times have you been on him?"

"At least a dozen. He's pretty smart. It only took him four days to realize what was going on. It takes most horses eight to ten. That fourth day, he kept my butt on the ground more than I kept it on his back."

Howard nodded. "You know, most people don't know it can take up to thirty days to break a horse. They watch the movies and see these guys buck and stomp a few times then ride away. It's an everyday challenge for weeks. Of course, it may only last twenty minutes a day, but your bones get to aching if you go much longer than that."

"Yeah, I know."

The older man chuckled. "Listen to me going on. I guess that's what you do when you get old."

Luke turned into the feed store lot. "All my life I wondered why I was drawn to horses, the rodeos, bull riding and such when neither one of my parents were interested. Then I met you." He glanced at the older version of himself. "As you said, 'like father like son.'"

A wide grin spread across Howard's mouth. "And I'm proud."

Samantha parked her red Mustang in front of Idaloo's. The business wasn't open yet but she knew Ben and Ida would be there preparing for the lunch rush. She hoped Aaron was there as well.

She went around the building and the back door stood open. She tapped her knuckles against the wooden frame of the screen and waited for an answer. Her stomach turned when Aaron appeared.

"Well, if it isn't Miss Hoity-Toity." He unlatched the flick lock and opened the screen door. "To what do we owe this visit?"

Sammi didn't step inside. "Are Ben and Ida here?"

"Why, you scared of me?"

Her heart pounded. She realized this was a mistake. "Never mind. I'll come back later." She turned to walk away.

Aaron grasped her arm. "Hey, wait a minute. I didn't say you could leave."

She jerked free of his hold. "I didn't ask."

Aaron grinned. "Uncle Ben and Aunt Ida are inside if you want to talk to them."

Facing him, she leaned to one side and glanced in the back door. "Ben? Ida?" she called. When she didn't receive an answer, she turned to leave.

⚜

"Beautiful drive through the canyon, isn't it?" Howard asked.

Luke slowed his speed when he entered the city limits of Lamoille. "Yes, it is."

"Want to stop at Idaloo's for a beer?"

"I don't think you should be drinking beer."

"Damn, an old man can't have any fun."

They passed through the tiny town quickly and soon approached the H-H land marker. "This is a big spread, Dad."

"Five thousand acres minus what I'm leaving Johnny

74

and Sam."

Luke's heart soared with pride then sank to the pits of hell when he recognized Samantha's red Mustang. It sat abandoned on the side of the road only a mile from the lane that led to the H-H ranch house.

CHAPTER 10

Luke studied the dirt around Sammi's car. "Doesn't look like there was a struggle."

Howard gave an affirmative nod.

"There's only one set of footprints and they appear to be Samantha's."

"Looks like she headed toward the house."

Luke walked back to the truck. "Let's hope so." He slid onto the driver's seat and put the pickup into gear. "I thought she had better sense than to go anywhere. Especially after yesterday. She's going to need a good excuse to get out of this one. I've a mind to bend her over my knee and teach her a lesson."

Howard chuckled. "Now that I'd like to see."

They arrived at the ranch house a few short minutes later. Relieved when he entered the kitchen and saw Samantha sitting at the table, he instinctively took her in his arms.

"Let me go." Samantha fought to free herself from his embrace. "What's the matter with you?"

Realizing the mistake he'd made by once again letting his emotions show, he released her. "Why is your car down on the road?"

"I—I loaned it to someone."

Lena's voice chimed in. "Sammi, you tell Luke the truth."

Samantha shot her mother a frown. "Alright. I ran out of gas, so what?"

"I thought I told you to stay on the property. Where did you go?"

"It's none of your business, Luke Dilashaw. You don't have the right to tell me what I can and cannot do."

"Do you realize the danger you put yourself in? Samantha, you could have been killed."

Samantha's heart fluttered at the sound of the words. Somewhat embarrassed that she was acting like a spoiled child again, she turned away. She knew she'd made a terrible mistake by leaving. She'd been scared to death walking home, and all she'd wanted was Luke's arms around her.

"I could have been killed, but I wasn't." Samantha noticed that Lena and Howard had quietly left the room. She was afraid her shield would crumble if he tried to hold her again. She had to get away from him. "Now, if you'll excuse me, I'm going to have one of the hands go get my car." She attempted to walk past him but stopped in her tracks when he stepped in front of her.

"Do you think this is some kind of game, Samantha? Well think again. It's serious."

She watched him pull something out of his pocket. "What's that?"

He unfolded the paper and handed it to her. "Another threat."

She went numb when she read the words. She stumbled backwards and sat hard in one of the kitchen chairs. "My, God."

"Sam, this is dangerous. They were only playing with

you yesterday. Now they mean business."

She studied the message. "Half-breed. I haven't been called that in years. Why are people so cruel?" Jumping at the sound of a heavy knock at the back door, she sprang to her feet when she saw Coke Johns round the corner.

Sammi threw her arms around Coker's neck. She could tell by the way Luke's jaw clenched that he fought hard to keep his composure.

"Oh, Coke, I've been a fool," she sobbed.

Coker embraced her and held her close. "It's okay, Sam, it'll be over soon. Trust me."

Luke met Coke's gaze. "I'll be in the study with my father when you're done here."

The sound of his boot heels against the hard wood floor became faint and she knew he was gone. She could stop acting now. Slowly she backed away from the sheriff's embrace. "Sorry, Coke, I guess I lost it there for a minute."

"That's okay, I liked it. Hey, we'll get this straightened out. I promise."

"The sooner the better. I have to get out of here before I lose my mind. I need to get back to work."

"Is your career suffering?"

"Not really. I made arrangements to be off for a month if necessary." She glanced down the hall where Luke had disappeared. But her emotions were in agony.

"I'm sorry your vacation turned out like this."

"Me too." Her time off had been torment from day one.

"Well, I'd better get to Howard's study and find out what this is all about." Coker turned to walk away.

"I guess so. See ya."

Howard stood and greeted the sheriff. "Come in, Coke, have a seat."

"Thanks, Howard. New problem?" he asked, sitting next to Luke.

"Yes." Luke handed the warning to Coke. "This was on the windshield when we left your place this morning."

"Why didn't you come back into the office?"

"We did, but you were already gone."

"Gone? I wasn't gone I was in the men's room."

How the man had gotten out of the office without anyone knowing had been eating on him. Knowing he was in the bathroom made him feel a little better. Luke watched as Coke read the words. "What do you think?"

"Looks like another threat to me."

Luke had a hard time holding his tongue. He wanted to lash out at the man's smart remark, or was it because Johns seemed to have the right to comfort Sam with his embrace any time he pleased? Either way, he found it harder every minute to like the sheriff of Elko County. He took the paper from Coke. "I think that's obvious."

"A little irritable today, aren't we?"

"You're damn right. Anything that has to do with Samantha's safety, I'm concerned about. Now, let's get down to business."

Luke's frustration mounted. Coke Johns appeared indifferent about the morning's events, and all *he* wanted to do was hold Sammi in his arms and protect her.

He walked across the property to the stables. The smell of straw, oats and horse droppings met his sense of smell. When he approached the black stallion's cubical, the horse became restless.

"It's okay, boy, I just want to ride you for a little while. You're going to let me do that, aren't you?" He doubted it. The stallion hadn't willingly let him on his back yet.

Luke retrieved a halter from the tack wall. He watched

the eyes of the big black horse dart from side to side in anticipation. Stepping inside the stall, he put the leather straps into place and fastened the buckle.

Holding the lead rope, Luke took the horse out of the stable and into the corral. The spring sunshine reflected off his shiny, ebony coat. "You're beautiful. I guess I should give you a name."

"Boy, he's slick and shiny, isn't he?"

Luke glanced up and saw Howard sauntering toward the corral. "He sure is. I think you just said his name. Slick. I like that."

"Seems to fit his personality and his look."

"Slick it is then. I'd better get a saddle on him and get this fight over with." He handed Howard the rope.

Samantha watched Luke and Howard from her bedroom window. Luke put the saddle blanket in place, then effortlessly lifted the heavy leather saddle onto the stallion's back.

His strength was unmatched by any man she'd ever known. Her blood surged with wanting while she watched his muscles flex under his tight fitting shirt as he pulled on his leather buckskin gloves, she realized she held her breath at the beautiful sight. Why couldn't she subdue these feelings?

The stallion fussed when Luke bridled him but stood perfectly still while Luke slowly mounted. Then, as if struck by a bolt of lightning, he started to buck, twist and stomp. Luke held on. It looked as if his knees bore holes in the horse's shoulders. One hand flung through the air while the other held on. His tall frame seemed to be made of rubber when it gracefully waved atop the stallion's back.

Minutes passed. She was amazed at Luke's stamina. Then her thoughts went back to his love making. He definitely had the power to endure in the bedroom. She shook the memory, and a small scream escaped her lips when Luke finally hit the ground.

He sat for short seconds then got up and brushed off his backside. Picking up his hat, he slapped it against his leg, replaced it on his head then climbed back on the stallion. Howard sat quietly on the top rail of the corral and watched his son at work.

Samantha knew the older man wished he could break the horse, but that is exactly what had caused his heart attack and Luke wouldn't allow him to take the chance.

The stallion leaped and bucked, tossing Luke around like a rag doll, but he persevered and finally succeeded in bringing his mount under control. She watched as he kept his place in the saddle and slowly walked the horse around the corral. Horse and man matched each other in strength and beauty. She longed to go outside and be a part of the excitement, but her pride kept her at bay.

CHAPTER 11

"Well, you did it for today. It only took you fifteen minutes this time," Howard said.

Luke smiled. "That's the shortest time yet." He gestured toward the corral gate. "Would you open that for me? I think I'll take him for a ride."

Howard hopped down into the dirt and walked to the gate. "Be careful. You never know when he'll take off on you."

"Yes, sir, I will." Howard was right, it could be dangerous taking Slick out of the corral, but he felt a bond with this horse he'd never experienced with any other. He trusted the steed.

He slapped the reins on Slick's hind quarter and the horse took off in a flash. They rounded the back side of the house and headed into the hills.

The wind whooshing past his ears made him feel carefree, but as he slowed Slick to a trot, his mind turned to Samantha. He was trying his damnedest to protect her. Why couldn't she understand that?

His comprehension of the female species, especially Samantha, was growing less and less.

The sun beat down on his bare shoulders. Wiping sweat from his brow, he rode through the sage covered hills and noticed a batch of trees down in a small valley. He decided to investigate the beautiful setting that was probably the land Howard had given Samantha. When he arrived at the bottom of the hill, he saw a trail leading into the sight. He followed the path and when he reached its end, splendor met his gaze.

Plush green grass covered the ground around a pond, which had been completely secluded by the trees and underbrush. Lily pads dotted the surface of the clear blue water, and cattails sprang up around parts of the border. Like a backdrop from a movie, it looked too inviting to be real.

He decided to take advantage of the cool water. Tethering Slick to a nearby branch, he discarded his boots and pants then splashed into the pond. The natural pool was refreshing when he swam across it, and he relaxed for the first time in days.

His mind wandered to Samantha and thoughts of how wonderful it would feel to have her warm naked body against his in the cool water. He envisioned her long black hair floating around him and her dark skin glittering with droplets. Imagining her firm bare breasts pressed to his chest caused a tightening in his groin, and he longed to hold her, feel her in his—.

"Hey, gold digger, you having fun?"

Startled from his thoughts, he quickly looked in the direction the voice came from. He could see no one. He swam to the shoreline where his clothes lay and started to get out.

"Don't get out of the water. I have a rifle pointed at your head. If you try anything, you're history."

His heart beat so hard, he feared it might jump out of his chest. He realized how vulnerable he was. Even if he could get to his clothes and his horse, he had no weapon except his bare fists. "What do you want?"

"It's simple. I want you to leave town."

"Why? Do I know you? Have I done something to you I'm unaware of?"

"Let's just say you have something that is rightfully mine, and I want it back. I could have had it no questions asked, then you had to show up. If you leave town and take that murdering half-breed with you, there'll be no more trouble."

Luke glanced down into the clear pool of water. His expression showed the anger he felt inside at the nasty remark the man made about Samantha. "Are you crazy? Samantha's not a murderer."

Hearty laughter come from behind the bushes. "You don't know, do you?"

"Know what, you bastard?"

"Oh, oh, oh, let's not get testy."

Luke shivered. The cool water that felt wonderful only minutes ago, now felt like a cold blanket of ice crushed against him.

"Don't forget who's holding the winning hand in this game."

For now, but I'll beat you before it's over. He had to make a move. His pulse pumped and the tingle in his fingertips stung his skin like pricks from a thousand tiny needles. "I'm getting out of this water whether you like it or not." He slowly rose to his feet then heard the deafening sound of a shot. A bullet whizzed past his ear and entered the water beside him.

Slick whinnied and reared up. He hoped he could calm the horse down before he got on his back again. Damn whoever was doing this.

"I won't miss next time, Dilashaw. Now let's get back to the topic of murder. Samantha Rainwater is a killer."

"She's never hurt anyone in her life."

"She killed her own father. In cold blood. Just shot him in the head and he fell over dead."

"If that was true, she'd be in prison." Laughter once

again emitted from the bushes.

"Yeah, if she'd been old enough to go to jail, but she was only six years old when it happened. She has the killer instinct, and we don't want her around these parts anymore."

A knot formed in the pit of his stomach. Poor Samantha. That must have been what her nightmare was about. Now he understood her warnings to stay away from her. *She thinks she's a murderer.*

"So, what about that? Killed her own flesh and blood."

"There's probably a good reason for what she did. And with the threats you've been making, you're no better than an assassin yourself."

"Dilashaw, you listen, and listen good."

There was something familiar about the way the man said his name, but Luke couldn't put a finger on it. He made a mental note of the sound of the voice. It might take him a while, but he swore he'd figure out the man's identity.

"Get out while you can. This is your last warning."

"Tell me what you want. Maybe we can negotiate."

Silence followed. Then the sound of running footsteps. Was it his imagination? Or did he hear more than one set of horse hooves pound the ground in a run? One horse went north, where the voice had come from, and it sounded like two horses rode south. Who else had witnessed this encounter?

Hurrying out of the water, he pulled on his clothes, approached Slick and managed to calm the horse before he hoisted himself into the saddle. Surprised the steed didn't protest the weight on his back as Luke reined him in the direction of the house. "I'll find out who that was, boy. No one threatens me and gets away with it."

"Howard, don't tell me that." Samantha hoped her tone didn't show disrespect, but she was frustrated. "You and my mother are both crazy." She shot a glance at Lena who stood behind Howard as he sat at his desk. She saw a smile lift the corners of the old man's mouth, and her first instinct was to turn and walk out of the room, but she couldn't.

Howard met Sammi's gaze. "You may not want to admit it, but there is something between you two. We can see it in your eyes and his."

Why did they insist on meddling in her private feelings for Luke? She took a seat in one of the chairs across from the couple she loved. "You are talking about me and Luke, but you two can't see three feet in front of your own faces. You've been in love for years."

Lena's face turned scarlet and Howard's eyes widened. Samantha fought the impulse to grin as her mother spoke.

"Young lady, you go to your room."

"Momma, I'm twenty-six years old."

Howard cleared his throat then shifted in his chair. "I don't care how old you are, do as your mother says."

Samantha allowed her smile to surface. She stood. "See what I mean? You act like an old married couple." The stern expression on Howard's face told her she'd said enough. "Okay, okay, I'll go."

She left the older couple to deal with the issue. Her soul soared at the prospect they might actually admit their love for each other.

She walked down the hall, glanced out the back door then stepped outside. Two riders quickly rode into the barn on their horses. She longed for a ride. Looking into the hills, she thought of her favorite place and how good a swim would feel right now. The small pond that had been her private paradise over the years was now hers. It sounded inviting.

After walking back inside, she filled a glass with ice, poured herself some lemonade then returned to the back deck and sat at the table. The cool liquid soothed her parched throat as she drank it down.

Sounds of hooves hammering against the ground caught her attention. Everyone seemed to be in a hurry to get back to the barn today. Her breathing all but stopped when she saw Luke's tall form round the corner astride the shiny black stallion.

Passion surged through her when she remembered the warmth of his skin against hers and his hard pec muscles pressed against her bare breasts. Why did these feelings continue to haunt her when she wanted so desperately to forget them? She wanted to forget him, and what his mere presence did to her. *You're in love, stupid, that's why.* She couldn't deny it any longer. Her mother and Howard were right.

She watched him ride his horse into the barn. Minutes later he strode toward her and stepped onto the deck. Her body throbbed with longing as he approached.

"Afternoon, Sammi."

His deep voice penetrated her soul when he said her name. "Luke." She couldn't meet his gaze.

"Mind if I have a seat?"

She felt reckless for giving into her emotions, but she wanted his company more than anything. She closed her eyes and willed her pulse to slow its pounding. "No."

She glanced up when Luke sat across from her. The tension was thick enough to be cut with a knife. His voice seemed strained when he spoke, and every muscle in his face was rigid. Something was wrong, very wrong.

CHAPTER 12

"**L**uke, what's happened?

He met her worried stare. She was beautiful. Every time he looked at her his feelings for her grew. He couldn't tell her what had happened. It would only worsen her fear, yet it might stop her from doing something that would put her in jeopardy. No, he wouldn't scare her.

"Luke?"

Unable to lie to her face, he glanced away. "I went for a ride and Slick threw me, that's all."

"Are you alright?"

"Yeah." He met her gaze. "Are you?"

"What are you talking about?"

He wanted them to be able to communicate without misunderstanding each other. The kiss from the evening before crossed his mind for the thousandth time. "After last night I thought we might—"

"Continue with the game?"

"Game?" Once again she apparently read something into his words that wasn't there. "I think—"

"Well, don't think anything about me. You don't know me and you don't want to."

His mind flashed back to the intruder's words, and sorrow gripped his heart. How could he make her correctly perceive what he was about to say? He came to the conclusion that being straightforward would cause the least confusion. "I know about your father, Sam."

Samantha couldn't believe her ears. *He knows?* Shame surged through her. Her chest tightened and she thought she'd be sick. Tears welled in her eyes, she felt ugly and violated. Now she understood why he'd pushed her away last night after she kissed him. The urge to get away from him overwhelmed her senses as she stood.

"Where are you going?"

Without an answer she veered around him to pass, but not far enough.

His hands circled her waist and pulled her to him. "I asked you a question."

She fought to keep from crying. "Please, just let me go."

"Sammi, I understand."

"You don't understand anything." She tore from his grasp, and her tears spilled. "You think you can protect me? Who's going to protect you from me? No one, Luke. That's why you stopped last night. You think I'll kill you, too."

"That's not—"

"Admit it. You're ashamed that you've made love to a murderer." She knew she was out of control, but she couldn't stop herself. "Go ahead, say it, Luke. That's what I am! A murderer!" Feeling as if she would explode with anguish, she turned on trembling legs and ran into the house.

Locking the door to her room, she flung herself onto her bed. Why? Why did it always come back to haunt her? The sound of footsteps met her ears. The tone of Luke's low soothing voice came through the door.

"Sammi, talk to me."

"Leave me alone."

"Please, Sam."

"Go away."

"Sammi, I—"

"I said, leave me alone!"

"Is that what you really want?"

No, that's not what she wanted, but it had to be. "Yes. Yes, that's what I want." Silence was followed by footsteps. This time they faded into the distance. He'd granted her wish and she allowed her tears to flow freely. He knew she was a killer and it broke her heart, but knowing she could never have the one and only man she'd ever love, shattered it to pieces.

The barn was quiet and Luke patted Slick on the rump. He had let the horse cool after their ride and now he needed to brush his back. Slick may not care if he was groomed, but the endeavor might help calm his own emotions.

He went to the tack wall and retrieved a brush. As he curried the stallion, he felt a bond. The horse was beginning to trust him, if only he could say the same about Sammi.

He didn't pity Samantha he was concerned about her. She'd been carrying the burden of her actions for a long time and he longed to help ease her pain, but if she wouldn't allow it, what could he do? When the time was right, he'd approach Lena and find out what exactly happened twenty years ago.

"Well, Slick, that woman has my world turned on its head and she misinterprets everything I say. Whatever happens we've got to protect her, boy." Luke brushed Slick's hind quarters. "She's been hurt enough for one lifetime."

Making his way to the back of the barn to get some oats for his new friend, Luke studied the grandeur of the building and the animals it housed. His father had done a hell of a job turning the ranch into a successful business, and he admired him for it.

He noticed the pair of horses that occupied the last two stalls, their backs marked with sweat just as Slick's had been. His stomach lurched as his mind flashed back to earlier at the pond. Could these be the horses he heard riding away? He knew their riders would come to take care of them, and when they did, he'd be waiting.

After rewarding Slick with oats, Luke went to the house, poured himself a tall glass of iced tea and proceeded out to the deck where he could watch the barn.

Time ticked by slowly, and dusk was just around the corner. If someone didn't show up soon, it would be too dark to see.

He heard the creek of the screen door and welcomed Lena's company. Noticing her petite frame and elegant features, it was clear where Sammi got her beauty but not her height. "Evening, Lena."

She smiled as she took a seat. "It's beautiful out here, isn't it?"

"Yes, ma'am."

Lena sighed. "I think we need to talk, son."

"Yes, ma'am, we do." The way she twisted the band on her finger told him the subject was as hard for her to discuss as it was for him to hear.

"I've never taken it off," she said, studying the gold ring. "My love for Samantha's father died many years before he did, but I couldn't bring myself to remove this. I fell in love again but...that never worked out."

Luke wondered if she was speaking of the obvious bond she had with Howard. He listened as she recalled the sordid events of twenty years ago.

"I was very young when I married. We were happy at first, but I noticed he couldn't keep a job and I was so naïve, in love or just plain too stupid to realize he was lazy and didn't want to work."

She swiped at a tear that rolled down her cheek. Luke

didn't want her to have to relive that time if it hurt her this bad. "You don't—" Her hand flew up and he knew that meant for him to be quiet, so he granted her wish and sat back in his chair.

"I went to work to supplement the income, but when he started drinking and spending the rent money, I began to pack up to leave.

"I'd been feeling sick in the mornings, but I thought it was my nerves." She smiled and glanced into the distance. "Not nerves...I was pregnant with my baby girl. It was the happiest, and sadist day of my life. What was I to do? I had to stay with Lance Calhoun."

"Calhoun? I thought his name was Rainwater."

Smiling she shook her. "No, that is my maiden name. After his death, I took it back and also legally changed Sam's."

That made sense now. He knew Samantha's father was white and he'd wondered why the man had an Indian name. "I understand. I like Rainwater much better. It fits you and Sammi both." He paused. "Could you have moved back in with your parents?"

She nodded. "Probably, but my father was very ill and my mother was his caregiver. It took every penny they had for medicine and hospital bills. I couldn't burden them with my problems as well. Besides, if I were to have left and Lance found out I was pregnant, there would have been hell to pay. Not that there wasn't anyway."

"I'm so sorry."

Meeting his gaze she said, "Don't be. It was a long time ago and because of what the Lord gave me, I'm here to talk about it."

He knew what she meant. The Man upstairs had put her in his life, too, but he'd messed it all up. "Samantha?"

"Yes." She inhaled deeply then let the breath out. "I did everything he wanted me to do while I was pregnant and he didn't beat me once. However, over the next six years, Sam saw more of that man's vile actions toward me then any little girl deserved." Tears spilled onto her cheeks again. "I shouldn't have put the little thing through that, but I was afraid for my life. Most of all, he'd threatened to kill my baby girl if I tried to leave. I just couldn't take the chance of something happening to her.

"Then one night his beating me was more than she could bare. I heard her tell him not to hit me again or she'd shoot him. He laughed and struck me with a blow that rendered me unconscious, so I don't know exactly what happened after that, but when I woke up, he was on the floor beside the bed a single shot to the head. Sam sat in the corner crying and held her favorite teddy bear."

"Oh, Lena." The pleading look in her eyes tore at his heart. When she finished, he went to her and held her. Her silent tears wet his shirt. What could he say? The truth was out. He wished he could do more than comfort her, but words couldn't erase the past.

"Don't give up on Sammi. She'll come around, she loves you, Luke."

She sure didn't act like it. But then, he wasn't exactly allowing his true feelings to show either. It was clearer every day that his love for her grew, no matter how hard he tried to stop it.

He now had a clear picture of the pain Samantha had carefully buried, the pain that must have tormented her night and day. He longed to protect her, comfort her, be with her. If she didn't want him, he wouldn't force his love on her, but he intended to clear the air between them. After that, the fate of their relationship would be in her hands.

Movement in the distance caught his attention. He continued to hold Lena but slowly turned his head, thankful the sun still peeked over the west ridge. Luke watched the two men enter the barn, their faces etched in his mind.

"What's this?"

He released Lena at the sound of Howard's deep voice

and tried to lighten the atmosphere. "Jealous, Dad?" She slapped his shoulder playfully.

"Mind yourself, young man," Lena scolded.

He watched a scarlet blush cover her cheeks and heard his father nervously shuffle his feet.

Howard cleared his throat. "Lena's right, don't be smart."

Luke smiled to himself. "Yes, sir."

Lena dried her tears with her fingers. "Well, I guess I'd better go fix us some supper. I'll call you when it's ready."

Shadows covered the porch as darkness fell, but Luke could still read the look on his father's face as he watched Lena walk into the house. "Why don't you tell her you love her, Dad?" His own words hit home, making him realize just how much he was like Howard Hale.

Howard took a seat. "Why don't *you* stay out of it?"

He laughed at the old man's playful tone but knew he'd meant what he said. The more serious issue of the afternoon's events caused the smile to fade from Luke's face. "Something happened today I think you should know about."

Looking at Luke, Howard asked, "And what might that be?"

Luke saw the two men walking away from the barn. He wanted to make sure his suspicions were right. "Wait here, I'll be right back."

When he returned to the porch, his hunch had been confirmed. He took a seat across from Howard. "While I was out riding Slick earlier, I had an encounter with someone." He watched a questioning look cross his father's face.

"Do you know this someone?"

He wanted to make sure everything was clear in Howard's mind before he exposed the names of the men. "Yes, I know who it is, but before I reveal that, let me tell you the whole story. I want to know if you think I'm right in my assumptions."

"Fair enough."

Sitting back in his chair, Luke related the events and watched his father's expressions change. The dim porch light did little to hide the anger on Howard's face as he told him about the two lathered horses in the barn. "They were dried by the time I saw them."

"How do you know who'd been riding them?"

"I stayed out here and watched two men go into the barn then come back out. That's what I just checked, the horses have been groomed."

"Okay. I think it's time you told me who these men are."

He hated to do it but knew he had to. "It was your brother Johnny and his friend Frank."

"Johnny. What the hell does he think he's doing. I'll go talk to him right now, you call the sheriff."

Luke grabbed his father's arm. "Wait, Dad. I think we should wait. Let all of this sink in, and rationalize what to do."

"Alright. We'll call Coke first thing tomorrow so he can—."

"There's no need to bring him into this if it's a family affair. Johnny's probably ticked because I got the ranch. He doesn't know about the land and money you're giving him. Let's take care of this privately. When it's cleared up, we'll tell Johns he can call off his investigation."

"Are you sure this is how you want to handle it?"

"Yes, sir."

Lena's voice echoed from inside the house. "Supper's ready."

Luke was pleased when Howard nodded his head in agreement.

In the safety of her room, Samantha argued with Howard through the door. "I'm not hungry."

"You've got to eat, young lady. Now, you have two minutes to get to the table. We'll be waiting."

"But—"

"No buts, Samantha."

She heard him walk away. Why did he have to treat her like a little girl? And why did he still have the same effect on her now as he did when she was a youngster? She had always respectfully done what she was told and found herself doing the same as a grown woman.

She brushed her hair and studied her reflection in the mirror. She'd slept hard after her afternoon cry, and her eyes were red and puffy. She didn't want Luke to see her like this. "Humph, why should I care what he thinks?" Throwing the brush onto the dresser, she realized the reason Howard had treated her like a child was possibly because she was acting like one.

The doorknob felt cold. Was it that or the thought of facing Luke that caused the chill to run up her spine?

Squaring her shoulders, she left the security of her room. The smell of tacos drifted through the hallway and made her realize how hungry she really was. When she turned the corner and entered the kitchen, all eyes focused on her.

Her knees became weak, and the sight of Luke's handsome face didn't help. His gray eyes were troubled. Was it anger, hate, or contempt she saw in them? She couldn't blame him for the way he felt about her now. She knew he'd never be able to accept a killer into his heart.

Bile rose in her throat, but she forced herself to swallow and took a seat across from the man she could never call her own.

Howard began to fill his plate. "It's about time. I'm starved."

Lena handed Samantha a basket filled with taco shells.

"Here, honey."

"Thank you, Momma." She took two shells, handed the basket to Luke and felt him flinch when their fingers touched.

Setting the container on the table he asked, "How are you feeling?"

She sneered at him. How could he act concerned after he all but admitted he detested her? "Fine, thanks."

Luke hoped after he had a talk with Sammi, her behavior would change. He just didn't know how to approach her. He did know, however, keeping her safe was his first priority. Having discussed it with his father, he was pleased they decided not to bring the sheriff into it.

Coker Johns rubbed him the wrong way. He couldn't put his finger on it, but there was something about the man he didn't trust.

The air in the kitchen was thick with tension. Everyone ate in silence. He glanced once again at the woman he'd first known as Rain Storm. Her excellent singing voice echoed in his ears. He'd love to hear her sing again. Before he knew it, his mouth worked faster than his brain. "Rain, would you sing for me tonight?" He watched her slowly lift her head and meet his gaze. Before she spoke, the look in her eyes gave him the answer.

Her brow furrowed. "How—"

"I shouldn't have asked."

Howard spoke between bites. "I'd love to hear you sing, Sam. You haven't hummed a note since you've been home."

"I'm sure Sammi doesn't feel like singing tonight," Lena said.

Luke was sorry he'd brought up the subject, but at least everyone was talking.

Samantha laid her fork on her plate and looked at Luke. "Maybe it would help me work out some of my frustrations. After we clean up this mess, I'll sing a few songs."

"Good, good," Howard boasted.

Luke continued to eat in silence. *But not before we get a few things straight between us, my little songbird.*

CHAPTER 13

Sammi went into her room to get her guitar. Lost in thought, she felt Luke's presence before she heard him. When she turned, he stood in the doorway determination marked his face. She made a futile attempt to pass him. "Excuse me."

He took her guitar and leaned it against the wall. "You're going to listen to me, Samantha."

"I think you made yourself clear earlier."

"No, you put words into my mouth. This time they're going to be my words."

He was so close the warmth of his breath brushed her lips. When she attempted to step backward, he caressed her shoulders.

"Come here."

His kiss was tender, and she melted into him. Why was he tormenting her so? Didn't he know she loved him and couldn't resist him no matter how he felt about her?

Luke lifted his lips from hers. "Did that feel like the kiss of someone who hates you?"

Afraid of losing the moment, she didn't open her eyes. "No," she whispered. He scattered tiny light kisses down her neck and heat rose in her blood.

"Does this feel like something I would do if I thought

you were evil?"

She could barely breathe. "No," she muttered. The tenderness of his mouth still lingered on her skin as he cupped her cheeks with his palms.

"Look at me."

She forced her lids open and met his smoldering gaze. Those were not eyes that detested her.

"Sam, we need to call a truce."

"A truce?" Her heart warned her of the danger.

He dropped his arms and took her hands in his. "Yes. I think we'll get more accomplished." He smiled. "You need to trust me."

She slowly let go of his hands. He was right, their bickering wasn't getting them anywhere. "Trust you? Okay, but first you have to answer a question for me."

He leaned against the door frame. "What's that?"

She swallowed the lump in her throat and forced out the words that had haunted her for months. "Why did you leave that way in Las Vegas?" His steel-colored eyes met hers and she held her breath. Did she really want to know?

"I didn't want to leave like that, but my feelings for you forced me to."

"Forced you?"

He pushed away from the door and stepped toward her. "Rain, I knew if I didn't get out of there, I couldn't resist you. You had an unexplainable power over me. My life was in an uproar, and I couldn't expose you to the consequences it could have brought."

Of course. That was just before he had come to meet Howard. He was uncertain about his future.

"Why didn't you simply tell me that?"

"Are you kidding? I didn't think Rain Storm would be interested in my private affairs. You're a star."

"I'm not a star, Luke, I'm Samantha. Samantha Rainwater. But then, you couldn't have known that. Rain Storm is someone I made up years ago. I have the talent to sing, but I couldn't bring myself to put it into motion. Rain Storm gave me the courage to move forward."

"Sammi, my leaving had nothing to do with anything you did. Every day we were together was perfect. It's a memory I'll cherish forever."

God how she'd longed to hear those words. For a moment their gazes locked. She wanted to leap into his arms, but she had to broach the matter of her father. She didn't want to, but it was important. Her stomach filled with butterflies as the memories of the event raced through her mind. She looked downward. "About my father."

"Your mother told me all about it. You were six years old, for God's sake. Your mother was about to lose her life." He tilted her chin upward. "You did the right thing. Stop thinking about it in a negative way. Positively, you saved your mother from dying at the hands of a mean and wicked man. You should get a medal."

His account of the ordeal made her smile. "Thank you. The night it happened there was a terrible thunderstorm. That's where my stage name came from. I thought I drew strength from the name Rain Storm. Now that I think about it, I guess I use it as a constant reminder of that night."

"In the future, use it as a reminder of the gift you've been given. Samantha Rainwater AKA Rain Storm, the man above gave you a beautiful voice. Besides saving your mother, you're the hero of thousands of fans."

She realized she had been blessed with a wonderful life despite her early childhood. A strange peace filtered into her soul. She would never think of herself as a hero, but she'd try her hardest to stop thinking of herself as a murderer.

Howard's voice rang cheerfully through the air. "Ya'll comin' out here any time soon? We're ready to hear some music."

Luke kissed her softly then leaned over and picked up her guitar. "We're on our way, Dad."

Suddenly, she felt like singing.

The morning sun streaming through the window, brightened the study. Luke stood by while his father sent word with one of the hands for Johnny to come into the house.

"Tell him not to be slow about it either."

"Yes, Mr. Hale." The man took his leave.

The expression on Howard's face told Luke he was angry and hurt. He wondered if the old man felt betrayed. He heard the sound of footsteps coming down the hall.

Johnny Hale stepped through the doorway. "You send for me, Howard?"

"Yes, I did. Have a seat." He gestured to the chair next to Luke.

"What's up?" Johnny asked as he sat down.

Howard leaned forward and propped his elbows on his desk. "Well, my brother, we've been having some problems around here."

"Uh, problems?"

"Yes, and there's evidence you may be involved."

When Luke spoke, he watched Johnny squirm in his seat. "Where were you yesterday afternoon?"

"Well, uh, I was in town most of the day."

Glancing at his father, Luke asked, "Doing what?"

"Now listen, young'un, what I do in town is none of your business."

"Answer Luke's question, Johnny."

Johnny glared at Howard. "I was—I was—. What the hell, am I a suspect here?"

Luke stood and walked to the window. "If you can prove you were in town yesterday, no." He turned back to face Johnny. "If you can't, well."

"Well, what?"

Luke stepped back over to the desk and leaned down to face Johnny eye to eye. "Let's cut through the dirt here. I know you were out riding horses with your friend, Frank, yesterday." Luke saw tiny beads of sweat forming above his uncle's top lip. "Want to tell me about it?" He returned to his chair and glared at his uncle.

"Wha...what gives you that idea?"

Luke's patience was growing thin. "Come on, Johnny, I saw the sweat-dried horses, and I know you and Frank went into the barn late in the evening and cleaned them up." Luke was surprised when he heard Samantha's voice.

"And I saw you two ride into the barn yesterday afternoon just minutes before Luke. You were in an awful hurry."

Luke smiled. *Perfect timing, Sam.*

Johnny got up and went to Howard. "I may have been out there, but I wasn't the one doing the shooting. I swear."

Sammi entered the room and took the chair Johnny had just left. "Shooting?"

Luke heard the alarm in her voice. "I'll explain later."

Howard addressed Johnny. "Then who was?"

"I don't know. I didn't see who it was. We were clear across the pond."

"What were you doing out there in the first place?"

"I—I went out there to put some scare into Luke, but someone beat me to it."

Hearing his name, Luke spoke. "What do you have against me?"

Johnny slammed his hand on the desk. "Hell, boy, I've put many a year in on this ranch, and it seems I'm going to lose it all to you. Someone who hasn't done a damn thing around here. You just stepped in and took over."

"So, you felt it necessary to threaten Sammi's life to make me leave?"

"I ain't tried to kill nobody. I only wanted to scare you away, but someone's been doin' it for me. Like I said, I didn't have nothin' to do with no shootin'.'"

Howard looked tired. Luke was concerned about his heart. He'd been through a lot in the last few days. "I think Dad needs to rest. Johnny, you and I will take care of this later."

"Wait, son, I want to tell my brother something." He cleared his throat. "Johnny, I haven't told you this in a long time, but I love you. I wouldn't depart from this world without leaving you something. You know that land you love so much in the west corner of the ranch?"

"Yeah."

"One thousand acres of it is yours."

Johnny sounded genuinely emotional. Luke glanced up to see tears well in his uncle's eyes.

"I didn't know, Howard."

"Well, you don't know this either. There's an account at the bank in your name. There's enough money in it to build you a nice house and get started with your own ranch. Now enough of this nonsense."

"Does this mean you forgive me for the trouble I've caused?"

"I should have told you about your inheritance sooner. I guess I can see where you'd be rankled some, but damn it, Johnny...oh what the hell, of course I forgive you, but you better ask your nephew and Sammi."

"Luke, Sammi, can you ever forgive me?"

Luke watched a tear mark the older man's cheek and knew Johnny was fighting for composure. He stood and approached his uncle. "It's over, Johnny, no real harm done. Go on now and start a new life for yourself."

Samantha gave Johnny a quick hug. "Forgiven. I wish you well."

Howard handed his brother a small gray book inside a clear plastic cover. "Here's the passbook to your money. You'd better get started. You have a lot to do."

Tears flowed freely down Johnny Hale's cheeks. Luke

felt sorry for the lonely old man as he gave his brother a bear hug.

As Johnny left the room, Luke came to the realization their problems were not yet solved. If Johnny Hale wasn't the one doing the shooting, who was?

CHAPTER 14

It was a nice morning and Luke was pleased that a week had gone by without incident. However, he was beginning to believe Johnny had lied about not being the one who'd shot at him and Samantha. How else would all of the turmoil have stopped at once. Still, he knew he had to keep his senses tuned to danger. He would never be able to forgive himself if anything happened to Sammi. Her sweet voice rang in his ears.

"It's beautiful out here, isn't it?" She took a seat in the Adirondack chair next to him.

"You're beautiful out here."

She smiled and glanced at him. "Luke, have you seen my mother or Howard this morning?"

He traced his memory. "No, as a matter of fact I haven't seen them since late yesterday afternoon. The last I heard, Dad told Lena to get dressed up, they were going to a dance." He saw mischief in Sammi's amber eyes.

"Those kids."

Luke laughed but soon his happiness faded. "They should have been home by now. Did you check your mother's room?"

"Yes. I assumed she'd already made her bed, but maybe it hasn't been slept in at all. Do you think they could have left earlier this morning to go into town?"

His stomach churned. "I don't know. Let's go check Howard's room and see if he slept in his bed last night." Samantha's soft footsteps followed behind him as he led the way into the house. When he placed his hand on the doorknob of his father's room, his pulse quickened. He prayed the old man's bed was in disarray.

Samantha placed her hand over his. "Luke, I'm scared."

He brushed her silky hair away from her face. "It'll be okay." Praying he was right, he turned the knob and pushed open the door. He smiled when he heard the ultimate sound of surprise in Sammi's voice.

"Mother!"

Lena was cuddled against Howard's chest, lovingly wrapped in his arms. Luke almost laughed. Lena resembled a child that had been caught with her hand in the cookie jar.

She looked up at her daughter. "Samantha!"

"Mother, what are you doing?!"

Luke grasped her arm when she started to enter the room. "Sam, maybe we should go." He glanced at the older couple. "I'm sorry I didn't knock first." He was happy they didn't catch the two making love.

She looked at him in disbelief. "Luke, they—."

"I know, and it's none of our business. Now, let's get out of here." Luke glanced at his father when he heard his voice.

Howard smiled and winked. "We'll be out shortly."

Luke marched Samantha into the hallway and closed the door. He glanced down and her eyes were like those of a frightened fawn. What was wrong with her?

Samantha tried to compose herself but her heart continued to pound. She felt the urge to run except her feet wouldn't move. Why was she feeling like this, and how could Luke just stand there? "I can't believe you're being so calm." She tried to wrench form his grip. "I'm going back in there and get my mother."

"Sammi, stop, they're over twenty-one. It's none of our business. Didn't you see the love in their eyes? Come on, let's go."

He was right, and she'd always wanted her mother and Howard to be together but something about seeing Lena in bed with him scared her. "I have to get her out of there." Luke's voice was smooth and soothing.

"What's wrong, Sammi? Why are you acting like a scared child?"

A scared child? Those words made her think, then she understood why she was so frightened. Memories of the last time she'd seen her mother in bed with a man were from the night she killed her father. "It's just…" She shook her head and forced the negative thought away and allowed the positive thought to take over, the night she saved her mother's life.

She took a deep breath. *Calm down. This is what you've wanted for years.* "Just…" It was ridiculous for her to react like that. She felt ashamed. More than anything, she wanted her mother to be happy. "Oh, never mind. You're right. For an instant I thought of…that night. But it's not that night and Howard isn't going to hurt my mother."

"So, you're okay?"

Her trembling began to subside, and her knees gained their strength back. "Yes. I'm good." She smiled and allowed her heart to fill with happiness. The couple had, after almost twenty years, finally realized their love for one another. "Let's leave the love birds alone."

Sammi followed Luke into the living room. Her spirit soared when she saw Howard and her mother nestled together on the couch. She let out a small chuckle at the sight of the two acting like teenagers in love for the first time.

Lena pushed away from him and straightened her dress. "Sammi, Luke, there's something we need to tell you two."

"I think we saw everything earlier, Mom, you don't have to tell us."

Howard raised his eyebrows. "Watch your tongue, Sam."

"Yes, sir." She sat down and gawked at the lovebirds across from her.

Luke sat beside her. "Did you two have fun at the dance?"

Howard pulled Lena close. "We didn't go to a dance, son."

"No?"

"No." He shifted on the sofa. "We went to the little wedding chapel in town."

Samantha saw her mother's love for Howard sparkle in her faded brown eyes, love hidden just below the surface for many years. "You two got married?"

Lena smiled and nodded. "We did, Sam."

Happiness touched every corner of Samantha's heart. Tears of delight wet her cheeks as she went to her mother.

She embraced first Lena, then Howard. "I'm so glad you finally saw the light."

"Speaking of light..." Lena held out her left hand.

Samantha studied the diamond ring on her mother's finger. "Oh, Momma, it's beautiful. And no one deserves something that precious more than you."

Luke crossed the room and shook his father's hand. "You did it, you old coot."

A grin lifted the corners of Howard's mouth. "Sure

did."

Awareness of the strong family love that hung in the air filtered joy through Sammi's being. "Howie, this means you're my daddy!" she squealed with pleasure.

"Yep, and Luke's your brother."

She turned to Luke and laughter bubbled inside her then escaped. "My, brother?"

Luke frowned. "And what's so funny about that?"

She tried to ebb her hysterics, but it was no use. Through her laughter she choked out, "Oh, nothing really. I've…just…never thought of you as my broth…brother."

❧

Luke loved to hear Samantha laugh. Her eyes frolicked with happiness, and she was ravishing. He had definitely never thought of her like a sister, but he did envision her as his lover. Maybe someday the time would be right for them.

"Well, sis, I'd say we have some celebrating to do. Why don't you go call Idaloo's and tell them there's going to be a party tonight?"

Sammi threw her arms around his neck. "I think that's a wonderful idea."

He enjoyed her spontaneous reaction and held her a moment longer than he should have. Her breasts pressed into his chest as he lifted her off the ground and lightly kissed her sweet lips.

Their smiles faded and he found himself barely breathing as he explored her expression. Did he see passion in her eyes? When he placed her feet back on the floor, it took all of his willpower to release her.

She wiggled free and the smile returned to her face. "I'd better make that call. We have lots of planning to do."

Luke shifted his gaze back to the happy couple. "What are you two staring at." He noted the teasing smirks on their faces.

"Did you see the sparks fly between those kids, Lena," Howard said, his gaze directed toward Luke.

"I sure did."

Howard looked over at his wife. "Maybe someday they'll see the light like we did."

"Maybe," she said.

Luke felt blood rush to his cheeks. He wished it was that easy, but he still hadn't made up his mind if he wanted to stay on the ranch or go back on the circuit. He swiped his finger across his mustache. "I'd better go tell the hands there's going to be a party."

Samantha held the phone receiver to her ear. "That's right, Ida. Mother and Howard tied the knot. "Yes, can you believe it?

"You're right, it is about time.

"I'm excited, too. Do you think you could clear a place for a band?

"Great. I thought I'd call some of my friends and we could enjoy live music.

"Sounds good to me, too, Ida. I'll see you soon." Samantha placed the receiver on the cradle just as Luke walked around the corner. "It's all taken care of."

"What do you need me to do?" he asked.

When she met his gaze, his silvery eyes burned a hole through her soul. "I think I can handle everything. I told Ida I'd help with the refreshments so I need to make a trip into town. Get a cake and a few other things. I'll be back soon." His closeness made every nerve in her body aware of her desire for him. "I'd better be going."

He grasped her arm when she turned. Heat spiraled through her. When she glanced at him she read concern in his eyes.

"I can't let you go into town by yourself. Don't forget, you might still be in danger."

Sammi had all but forgotten about the events of the week before. Things had been so pleasant she wasn't reminded. She eased her arm from his grasp. "You might be right. I'll get one of the hands to go with me."

"No. I'll go."

All week he'd been breaking horses and spending most of his time working around the ranch. It hadn't left much time for them to be together and she'd been glad. Her emotions skyrocketed when he was near, and she found it hard not to make a fool of herself, as she'd done only minutes earlier. "You don't have to go."

"I know. I want to go."

"Well, if you want to, I guess it's alright. I'll get my things."

"I'll get the pickup."

After Samantha stepped into the cab of the truck, Luke shut the door behind her. She watched him walk in front of the pickup. His tall frame moved with the grace of a lion as he made his way around. When he opened his door, he took off the Silver-belly hat he always wore, and set it upside down in the seat between them.

She saw his lean muscles flex when he stepped up into the driver's seat. A whiff of his spicy aftershave reached her nostrils and she closed her eyes. This trip into town could be torture. She jumped and opened her eyes at the sound of his low-pitched voice.

"Are we ready?"

She fought to keep her voice steady and light. "I think so."

"Then let's do it." He put the vehicle in gear and drove down the lane.

"Do you think we could stop at Idaloo's on the way? I'd like to check my list with Ida."

"No problem. I'd like to see the place anyway. I've

never been inside, just heard good things about it."

"You've never met Ben and Ida?"

He accelerated and pulled onto the road. "Nope."

"You're going to love them. They're great folks. Been out here at least a hundred years."

"And they're still walking."

"Okay, maybe not quite that long."

The ride to the small bar went by in a flash. Luke pulled into Idaloo's parking lot and her stomach knotted. She hadn't been there since her encounter with Aaron.

Just days ago, after she ran out of gas, on her walk home she remembered Aaron was afraid of guns. She knew he couldn't have been the one who shot at her. Still, hopefully, the creep wouldn't be there today.

"Sammi, what's wrong? You're awfully serious."

She forced a smile. "Oh, nothing."

Inside the tavern, Ben greeted them at the door. "Well, well, well. I hear we have reason to celebrate. You kids got married on us, did ya?"

Sammi felt every muscle in her body become taut. She glanced at Luke. Amusement marked his face. "No, Ben. It was Mother and Howard."

"Howard and Lena? Well, it's about damned time."

Ida came through the doorway from the kitchen wiping her hands on her apron. "Sammi, I'm so excited. I can't wait until tonight. I've told everyone. We're going to have a great crowd." The older woman eyed Luke. "And who is this handsome fella'? New boyfriend?"

Samantha gritted her teeth. Why did everyone try to put them together? "No, Ida. This is Howard's son. Luke Dilashaw."

Ben offered Luke a handshake. "So, this is the young man all the ladies have been talking about."

Ida pushed past her husband and hugged Luke. "I should have known. You look like your daddy." She backed away. "My, my, but I don't remember Howard Hale ever being quite as attractive as you are." She grinned and winked at him. "You better save a dance for this old lady tonight, you hear?"

Luke smiled and tilted the brim of his hat. "Yes, ma'am."

Samantha looked on as the older couple made over Luke. He was handsome, and incredibly sexy. The twinkle in his eye and the little grin on his face when he tilted his hat toward Ida, almost made her knees buckle with want. How could such simple things cause passion to take over her reasoning? She felt Ida's warm hand on her shoulder.

"Sammi, are you with us?"

"Sorry. What did you say?"

"Is this area over here all right for your musician friends?"

"Yes, that will be perfect."

"We'll cover the pool table and use it for the food."

"That sounds wonderful."

CHAPTER 15

Luke left the women to make their plans and followed Ben Wiley around the bar and into the small kitchen. Ben busied himself with preparations for the evening.

"What do you think of our Lamoille Canyon, young Mr. Hale?"

"It's Dilashaw, sir."

"Dilashaw?"

"My name. It's Luke Dilashaw."

"Oh, that's right. At my age, you become forgetful."

Forgetful the man might be, but he was still full of spunk. "I love it."

"Love what?" Ben asked.

"Lamoille Canyon."

"Oh, yeah. See what I mean. The mind just goes. Where, I don't know."

"I like your place."

"It's old like mother and me, but it's ours. We're about to retire you know."

"That's great."

"Yeah, well, I'm not sure about that. But in any case, my nephew is going to take over for us." Ben met Luke's gaze. "He's a city-slicker. Too bad he couldn't be a little more like you. Looks like you fit in real good around here."

"Thanks."

"If it don't work out with the nephew, the little lady that helps us out now and again wants to buy the place. That's our plan B, as they call it."

Samantha entered the kitchen. "Luke, we'd better go. I have a list a mile long."

Stepping toward her, he placed his arm around her small waist. "Whatever you say." He heard the screen door open and watched anger cross Samantha's face. When he turned, he met the gaze of a man who reminded him of...Elvis?

"Aaron, I'm glad you're here," Ida said. "I want you to meet Luke. This is Howard's son."

Keeping a protective arm around Sammi's waist he greeted, Elvis, without a handshake. "Nice to meet you."

Aaron nodded.

Luke felt Samantha tense when Aaron directed his attention to her. He didn't like this guy a bit and was incensed when he walked around Sammi and gawked at her backside.

"Mmm, Sammi, you're still looking good. I haven't seen you in a while. Miss me?"

Samantha turned and stepped toward Aaron. "Kiss my foot, Aaron!" she said then walked out of the room.

Ben grabbed his nephew's arm. "Watch your manners, boy."

Luke battled his temper. He didn't want this day ruined by the likes of this Elvis wan-a-be. He narrowed his eyes, glared at Wiley and inched his way closer and closer to the oaf's face.

"Yes, watch your manners. And tonight, stay away from Samantha. I'll have my eye on you. If you do anything to spoil the evening, you'll answer to me." He stood his ground while Aaron backed away.

Satisfied he'd made his point, he addressed Ida and Ben. "I'm sorry about this."

116

Ida took Luke's arm and led him out of the kitchen. "Don't you worry about it. Ben's brother did teach the boy how to be polite, but he and Sammi have had an ongoing feud for years. I'll make sure he's not here tonight then we won't have any trouble."

Sammi would appreciate that, and so did he. "Thank you, Mrs. Wiley."

"Now you two go into town and have fun. Don't let this put a damper on your day."

"Yes, ma'am."

Samantha breathed a sigh of relief when Luke came out of Idaloo's with nothing askew. She had felt his grip tighten around her waist when Aaron spoke to her. Afraid of what he might do, she got out of there as soon as possible. He started the pickup and put it in reverse. She saw the muscles in his jaw tighten and release.

"How long have you known Elvis?" he asked

She bit her lip and tried not to laugh. "Elvis?" Unable to stop her chuckle, she placed her hand over her mouth. His mood seemed to lighten as he aimed a questioning glance at her. "Most of my life."

"Has he always been a jerk?"

"Yes. We've never gotten along."

"Why didn't you tell me about him? He could be the one who's doing the shooting."

Samantha thought of her confrontation with Aaron the week before. "No. He's scared stiff of guns."

"Figures. But everyone grows up and most overcome their fears."

She'd never thought about that, but it was still hard for her to imagine Aaron the culprit. Feeling the need to lighten the atmosphere she said, "And, I know it's hard, but try not to associate him with 'The King'. Elvis is one of my heroes."

"Mine too, but Wiley really reminds me of him. Does he sing?"

She began to laugh. "He can't carry a tune in a bucket. The only thing he's ever been able to do well, is be obnoxious."

"He is that. So. you don't think he's had anything to do with the problems at the ranch?"

"Honestly, no."

"Okay. Let's forget it for now and concentrate on the party."

She could tell by the look on Luke's face it was all but forgotten. "Okay. First stop; the bakery."

Luke turned on the radio. "Any particular station you'd like to listen to?"

She glanced down at the numbers on the dial. "This one's, my favorite."

"They should be playing your music on here. Why haven't you ever made a record?"

"I've been in the studio a number of times, but only to do demos. I've always wanted to cut an album. What I'd really like is to be a producer. Owning my own recording studio is one of my dreams. I don't want to be a star so much as I'd like to help others become famous. I've studied the recording business for the last few years."

Luke glanced at her. "I'd think you'd have to be a genius to run one of those big things with all the knobs."

"It's a sound board. You don't have to be a genius but you have to understand the way it works. And most important, you have to know sound."

"You have been doing your homework."

Maybe one day her dream of having her own studio would come true. She would much rather do that than be on the road. "Oh, turn here." She pointed to the right. "The bakery's just down there."

The aroma of cinnamon, maple and fresh baked bread drifted on the air, as Luke followed Samantha into the small gourmet pastry shop. She did have a nice backside and he didn't like other men looking at it, especially not Aaron Wiley.

"Good morning, folks, may I help you?"

Sammi stepped toward the counter and spoke to the clerk. "We need to order a wedding cake."

"You two are going to take the big plunge, huh? Well, we've got a nice variety of cakes for you to choose from. When's the big day?"

Luke smiled at the question. It had been assumed so many times he and Sammi were the happy couple, he was beginning to enjoy it, but apparently, she wasn't. She shifted her weight from one foot to the other. He couldn't give her a chance to flail her frustration at this innocent soul. One pace forward and he was beside her. "It's not for us. It's for our parents."

The lady picked up a picture album and laid it on the countertop. "Oh, I'm sorry. You two make a perfect couple so I assumed...Well, here are some photos of cakes we've done in the past."

Samantha opened the book and studied the images. "I like this one," she said and pushed the book toward Luke.

"That's a nice-looking cake."

"We'll take one like this." Samantha pointed to the photo.

"When do you need to pick it up?"

"This afternoon. If you don't mind."

"Only two layers. You're in luck, honey. I don't have a thing to do today and I've got help coming. I'll spend all my time on your cake." She glanced at her watch. "It's eleven o'clock now. I can have it ready for you by two thirty."

"That's perfect," Sammi said. "We have some more things to do."

The time went quickly. Luke hadn't spent a day shopping with a woman since he was a child. He didn't remember it being fun, but now, with Samantha, he enjoyed it. Or was it her company he fancied? She made him happy he knew that. If he thought she'd settle down with him, he'd make the decision to stay at the ranch. *Don't get any big ideas, Dilashaw.* The mood of the event must be getting to him.

"Let's go into Steelman's western wear. I'd love to have a new dress."

He saw the gleam in her eyes. She was like a kid in a candy store. When they went inside, the smell of leather caught him off guard until he looked up. In a loft above the main floor, he saw men at work making saddles. "I didn't know they had a leather shop here."

"It's a couple of the local leather experts who make their wares, and sell them here. Saddles, boots, purses, that kind of stuff."

"I like that idea. Handmade saddles. I think I'll go take a look." Instinct prevailed and he bent and gave Sammi a fleeting kiss on the cheek. "Be right back." He was amazed at how natural being with her had become.

Sammi watched Luke walk up the stairs. The warmth of his lips lingered on her face. All this fuss over wedding things made her more aware of her longing to settle down. The years she'd spent fearing relationships still held their place inside her. It was hard to let go of the habit, but the longer she was around Luke the easier it became. She only wished the feelings were mutual.

Although he did seem to be in an exceptionally good mood. The kiss came out of nowhere, and the affection it carried felt genuine. Could it be he did have feelings for her? She'd give a million dollars to know. She lifted her hand to her cheek and with her fingertips, caressed the spot his lips had touched. If it were only that simple.

"Sammi?"

She dropped her hand from her face and glanced up.

"Coke, it's good to see you under happy circumstances."

"What's the special occasion? I saw Dilashaw's truck out there loaded to the gills."

"We're having a wedding party."

"Wedding? Are you and Dil—"

"No, silly. Mother and Howard ran off and got married last night." She couldn't explain the initial expression on Coker's face, but it wasn't one of joy. Suddenly, as if it were an afterthought, he smiled.

"That's great. So, you're having a celebration tonight?"

"Yes. At Idaloo's. Please come, Coke. It's going to be a great party."

"Don't look for me. I'm on call tonight. Tell the happy couple congratulations."

"I will." She watched him walk out the door. He was acting strange. What was his problem?

"Was that Johns?"

Lost in thought, she jumped at the sound of Luke's voice.

Apprehension flashed in his eyes. "Are you alright?"

"I'm fine. You startled me that's all, and yes, that was Coke. Why do men always use last names when they talk about someone?" A shrug of his broad shoulders was his answer.

"What did he want?"

"He saw your truck and wondered what was going on. When I told him about the party, he acted kind of..."

"How?"

"I don't know. Shocked maybe?"

He laughed. "The look on your mom's face this morning when we opened the door? Now that was shocked." His face grew somber. "I wonder if the sheriff has visited Norma's lately?"

"Norma's?" Why would he think Coke visited the brothels?

"Never mind. Is he going to be at Idaloo's?"

"He's on call tonight."

"Good."

"Don't you like him?" It wasn't dislike she read on Luke's face it was distrust. Why did every man who gave her a second look, or any attention at all for that matter, make Luke uneasy?

CHAPTER 16

Samantha greeted guests while her mother and new stepfather mingled. Ben was his old self behind the bar and Ida beamed from ear to ear. Everyone seemed to be in the mood to celebrate.

This was also a great opportunity for Luke to get acquainted with Howard's friends and business associates. She had accepted the fact Luke had taken over the ranch. Howard needed the rest and she was ashamed at her own selfishness in trying to keep him from relaxing in his golden years. He and Lena deserved happiness and she was glad they would enjoy the rest of their life together.

She glanced up to see Luke making headway through the crowd toward her. Love tugged at her heart strings. He was the one she would like to live out her life with, but their differences were too great.

When he approached, her blood pumped untamed through her body. Passion stirred and filled her with warmth and want for the attractive, strong yet sensitive, Luke Dilashaw.

It had to be the atmosphere that caused her to be so responsive to his presence. The lights were dim, the musicians played a slow waltz and as he got closer it seemed the room belonged only to them. It was reckless, but she couldn't stop herself. She had to be close to him, feel his arms around her. "Want to dance?"

"I'd love to." he replied.

The waltz was her favorite, and Luke had mastered it to perfection. His steps were smooth, precise, and they seemed to float with the beat of the music. One, two three. One, two three.

He held her close as they glided around the dance floor. She belonged in his arms. Their body's molded together as they had months ago when they'd made love. She closed her eyes.

Luke's warmth radiated through her. His hand on her back felt as if it would burn through her dress. His lips gently touching her cheek reminded her of every kiss he'd given her. Chills of excitement skipped up her spine. She was under his spell.

He stopped moving and when she opened her eyes, she realized the song had ended. Still wrapped in Luke's arms she glanced about the room. They were the only ones on the dance floor. The others stood around the edge smiling and looking at them.

Luke whispered. "Thank you."

Still resting in his embrace, she directed her gaze back to his. He bent his head and his lips brushed hers. Was he crazy? Everyone was gawking at them. He released her and a burst of applause came from the crowd.

"Wonderful," someone shouted.

"Beautiful," another boasted.

"You two were made for each other."

Heat rushed to her face. She had to get out of the center of the floor. As if her feet were filled with concrete, she couldn't seem to move. Luke's arm encircled her waist and she was thankful when he helpfully pried her from her position then led her to a chair. Was she in shock? Why else would she be acting like this?

She sat down and realized Luke still held her hand. She

watched as he knelt to one knee beside her.

"Are you alright?"

She seized a calming breath. "I guess so. How embarrassing." The glint in his eye suggested he was encouraged by the ordeal.

"I enjoyed it. Want to do it again?"

"Not on your life." That wasn't true. She'd love to do it again. In the privacy of her bedroom, but that was out of the question. It was only the mood of the celebration making him act so interested. Not her.

She scanned the room. To her relief, the people had focused their attention elsewhere. "I need a drink."

Luke stood. "I'll get you one. What would you like?"

"Lite beer's fine." She watched him walk away. What had she been thinking? She should have known asking him to dance would lead to calamity. It was hard enough to control her desire when she was simply close to him, much less while in his embrace.

"Here you go." Luke handed her a glass.

"That didn't take long." She looked up at his towering physique. "Thanks." He resembled a princely giant who had come to rescue his sleeping beauty. How she wished this were a fairy tale and he could whisk her away to live happily ever after.

"Sammi, you're staring at me." He set the drink down, took her hand, drew her to stand in front of him and studied her face. "What's behind that look you're giving me?"

"I—I'm sorry. I didn't mean to be rude." Afraid he might see her love for him hidden in the depths of her eyes, she shifted her gaze and withdrew her hand from his. "The band sure sounds good."

"Yes, they do."

She was abated when he didn't pursue the sensitive issue. He may have been impassive about it, but she knew she wouldn't be able to hold up under his scrutiny. His eyes were yet another one of her weaknesses. Would she ever stop being enchanted by this Prince Charming?

Ida approached them. "Sam, everyone's asking if you'll sing a few songs."

"Oh, Ida, I don't know." She hadn't quite calmed down.

Luke placed his finger under her chin and lifted her face so their gazes met. "Please?"

How could she resist that sexy smile? "Alright." She glanced at the older woman. "Okay, Ida. I'll sing." She watched Ida walk toward the band and wondered if the sweet lady knew it was Luke's plea that persuaded her decision.

"Folks. Folks, could I have your attention?" one of the musicians requested over the microphone. "I'm sure you all know we have a special guest in the house tonight."

The whistles, whoops and applause warmed Sammi's heart. She loved these people.

"Would everyone please welcome Rain Storm? Better known to us as Sammi Rainwater!"

❧ ☙

While Samantha went to the stage, Luke explored the faces of the cheering crowd. People had adoration in their eyes. His devotion to Samantha grew deeper every minute.

Not wanting to miss any of her performance, he sat on a stool, leaned against the bar and settled in.

She took her place behind the microphone. "Hi, everybody. Thanks for coming tonight. How about those kids Howard and Lena?"

Everyone shouted their approval. He thought the older couple looked like teenagers who'd discovered love for the first time. It was possible. He was close to thirty and just finding out what true love really was. And she was standing in front of him now, about to sing to her fans.

"Don't you think they make a great couple?" she asked

of the audience.

He freed his mind of his surroundings and concentrated on Samantha. Her shiny hair was so dark it glowed the color of indigo under the lights. Her eyes were bright with joy, and the body that lay beneath her clothing called out to him, "Hold me, touch me, love me."

It was time to face the truth. He'd denied his love long enough. Whether she knew it or not, she loved him too. He could see it in her eyes, feel it in her touch.

Her voice rang through the air. It's pure, rich sound touched his soul. She was in her element and he appreciated it. He wished he could make her dreams come true. Maybe someday she'd get the recording studio she wanted. She deserved it.

"Luke?"

He turned at the sound of Lena's voice. "Hi."

"She's wonderful, isn't she?"

"More than that."

"I came to tell you that as soon as she's finished, your dad and I are going to sneak out."

A slight red glow covered Lena's face and Luke smiled. "I see."

"We want to be alone."

"I understand." He wanted to be alone with Sammi.

"We're going to go into town and get a room. I hope you don't mind taking care of the ranch for a couple of days."

"Mind? Not at all." This would be the perfect opportunity for him to convince Samantha, she loved him. "I think it'll work out." Lena's expression told him she understood.

"Great. We'll check in from time to time."

"See that you do, young lady," he said with a smile. Samantha's words drew his attention back to the makeshift stage.

"I'd like to sing this next song for a special friend."

Luke's gaze locked with Samantha's. Her eyes were filled with love.

Samantha lowered her tone. "I think you know who you are."

Those were almost the same words she used when she sang to him in Vegas. Funny how she made him quake inside.

"This one's called 'Ride the Storm'."

"I think she means you, Luke," Lena said.

He nodded and listened to the words of the song as Samantha's voice rang through the quiet crowd.

"Ride the storm little one... it might be hard to do... the rain won't last forever... the thunder will fade too... you saved a life that fearful night... when you were so young... "

The song went on and now Luke understood the meaning of its words. After her father's death, Samantha's life had been filled with fear. He couldn't imagine what turmoil the woman had carried deep in her heart all these years. One thing was for sure, he hoped he could lessen her anxiety, help her move on and leave those fears behind.

Tonight was a good time to start. His mind was made up. Life on the rodeo circuit was no longer for him. Samantha. This life, here, in this little community, was what he wanted. He was sure of it.

Samantha studied the room of people. Where were her mother and Howard?

She approached Luke. His smile was bewitching. The force that surrounded him was unmatched by anything she had experienced. "Have you seen, Mother?"

"Yep."

He just kept smiling at her. What was he up too? "Well, where is she?"

"She and Howard went into town—to get a room—for two days."

"Two days!" Would she ever be able to resist Luke's power for that long? Doubtful. She'd have to get away as well. "I—I guess I'll stay with a friend until they come home."

Still cocked against the bar, arms folded, he addressed her matter-of-factly. "You know I can't let you do that. You may still be in danger. I have to protect you."

"Protect me? From who, you?"

His mouth drew into a grin. "I think it's too late for that."

He unlocked his arms and embraced her. She wanted to protest, but every part of her body rejoiced with his touch and she couldn't move. His gray eyes probed into the bottomless pit of her soul. She knew he could read her every thought and she didn't try to fight it.

Her battle was lost. He knew she loved him.

Their lips met in a kiss that sent jolts of electricity through her. The thump of her heart was surely loud enough for all to hear, but she didn't care. She was in love. When their lips parted, she could hardly breathe.

Luke whispered into her ear. "Let's go home."

When Luke pulled the pick-up onto the H-H lane, Samantha thought she would swoon with anticipation over what was about to happen. The early morning hours promised passion. Something she thought she'd never again experience. That wasn't true. She felt it every time she looked at the man who sat next to her at this moment.

They hadn't spoken a word since they left Idaloo's, but that suited her fine. She knew she'd be a babbling idiot if she tried to express her feelings with words.

Luke eased the truck to a stop and shut off the engine.

"You ready to go in?"

It was almost impossible to take a breath, and her heart, would it ever stop its stupid pounding? Damn him for doing this to her, but she loved it.

He faced her. "Sam, you all right?"

All she could muster was a nod. She wasn't all right. She longed to be in his arms. The thought made her shiver.

"Come on, you're getting cold." Luke got out and walked around to her side.

When he opened the door, she gazed into his moonlit eyes. Could he see she was anything but cold? The gentle caress of his hand on her elbow only caused the fever to rise. She didn't understand what force he held over her, but she knew she couldn't contest it.

Her mind was made up. All she wanted was to hear three simple words escape his lips. If he said them, she would stay on the ranch. If he couldn't tell her he loved her, she wouldn't force him too, and she would leave.

CHAPTER 17

She watched him open the ranch house door. He stood back to let her enter first. When she walked past, he tenderly turned her to face him, leaned her against the door frame and kissed her. She realized it wasn't the time to think of the future. This moment was what she'd longed for, and she wanted to savor every second.

Luke led her to her room, and before she knew it, their clothes had drifted to the floor. His skin was warm and smooth when she laid her hands on his flat stomach. How long she had yearned to be here.

Her tongue played in circles on the tanned skin of his chest, and the flavor of spice and salt drifted across her taste buds. "Mmm." *Uniquely, Luke.* Something she'd never forget.

If she could ever love a man for a lifetime, it was this one, but could he love her? His silver eyes were filled with desire and caused her to melt closer into him. Her bare bosom pressed against him, and hunger spread through her.

She watched him lean forward, and breathing became difficult when his hands cupped her cheeks. His lips brushed hers with one slight kiss, then another. "You're torturing me." And he was, but it was bliss.

"No more than you are me." He sank to one knee.

The heat from his fingertips remained on every place he touched, then the skin on her sensitive nipples threatened to sear when he gently caressed each peak. How could she have deprived herself of love for so long? His love. It took a special man to break the barrier, and Luke was him. She never dreamed she would cherish a man like she did the cowboy before her.

In the dim light that streamed through the curtain, she saw his gaze devour her nakedness. In no way had she felt so at ease with a man. He was her missing link and, now that she'd found him, could she ever let him go? She refused to think about what lay ahead. Tonight was what she wanted, no matter what.

She grasped soft locks of his hair as she looked down at him. Gazing into his gray eyes as he watched her, she was sure her heartbeat echoed through the hills outside. His lids closed and she smiled when he tickled her with his mustache.

Her flesh consumed the heat of his kisses that burned the way to her nipples. His lips covered first one then the other. The flick of his tongue caused her lust to run rampant. How did he do this to her? He awakened feelings she never knew she had. Luke Dilashaw was all she ever needed.

"Your skin feels like satin against my lips."

The sound of his voice made her longing grow more passionate. She fought the urge to beg him to take her at that very moment. He possessed the ability to make her lose control, but she had to hold on. She wanted this night to go on forever.

Chills danced up her spine when his mouth left her breasts, and his fingertips traced a trail then settled on her waist. The love in her heart was unbridled when he rose to his feet and claimed her lips with his.

His mouth was soft and she welcomed the eager exploration of his tongue. The heat of the kiss penetrated the very core of her being. He was her soul mate. She knew it, but did he feel the same way? Did he blaze inside like she did? His desire, hard against her stomach, added to the fire and told her he did.

When she wrapped her fingers around his velvet-covered hardness, a moan escaped his throat. He couldn't know what his response did to her, but her urgency was unbearably wonderful. It had been so long. Too, long. "Luke," she whispered.

He stood, lifted her into his arms, turned and walked a few short steps to the bed. He lay her on the soft mattress and took his place beside her. It was where he belonged, where she belonged.

Awed by his raw power, she couldn't help but wonder how such a virile man could be so gentle. As they lay facing each other, the length of their bodies welded together, she trembled. He was opening new emotions inside her she welcomed. When his hand trailed down her back and came to rest on her behind, the rhythm of his heartbeat quaked through his chest and hammered against hers, or was it her heart that drummed the cadence?

Luke's lips softly touched her ear as he whispered, "You feel so good. I've dreamed of making love to you at least a million times."

Tilting her head back, she studied his strong features. He was the most gorgeous man she'd ever known. "A million?"

"Maybe more," he answered huskily.

How could she ever live without him? But if she had to she...No, she wouldn't ruin her happiness. This beautiful man was hers for the moment and that's all that mattered.

His shoulder length hair lay across his neck in tousled tendrils. A strong brow marked his forehead, and eyes the color of a silver coin gazed back at her. She traced the bridge of his straight, defined nose with her finger. Perfect. Everything about him was perfect, and she'd known it the first time she laid eyes on him. Her thumb stroked gently across his mouth. "Then do it, Luke. Make my fantasies come true."

Their lips met and Luke tightened his embrace. Her skin tingled when he pressed his knee against her thighs. He was her fantasy. She wanted him, loved him and burned with desire when she opened to him.

To no avail, she tried to control her sporadic breathing. A stinging sensation lingered each place his mouth pressed against her skin. How could he bring such feelings to the surface when she'd worked her whole life to bury them? She didn't know and didn't care. The ache deep inside caused her to arch against him.

Luke had always made her feel things she couldn't explain and now was no different. He suckled aroused nipples and his hand pursued a course that led him to her wet folds. She felt she was suspended in an abyss of passion with the man she loved, and she wanted to stay a lifetime.

When he rubbed her most tender spot, her heart thumped and she couldn't control the wanting to rotate her hips in rhythm with his motions. She craved him so desperately she was going out of her mind.

Lifting her bottom slightly off the bed, she pushed against his hand. Surely, he wouldn't let her suffer much longer. She had to have release. Relaxing, she placed her palms on his broad shoulders and applied a gentle pressure that coaxed his mouth from her breasts. It staggered her that she could be so suggestive, but at that moment she had no qualms about letting him know what she required.

When he gazed up at her, she could see by the look of pleasure on his face, he was happy with her request. The dim light didn't conceal the message she tried to relay.

"You're a hell of a woman," he murmured, then planted kisses down her stomach that took root lower.

He was so sensitive to her needs. She only hoped she

would be as sympathetic to his, but right now, she needed him to take her to the highest realm. Opening herself completely, she allowed him to expertly carry her up the towering mountain of love. Her stomach muscles tightened, and waves of warmth washed over her when his tongue toyed with her delicate need.

She clenched his hair with her fingers when the swells of the tide became too frantic and battled the words that threatened to spill from her mouth. Only in her mind could she say them. *I love you. Oh, how I love you.* Her body trembled and her breath caught in her throat when Luke's warm mouth caused the waves to crash to shore in spasms of rapture.

Luke tasted Samantha's sweet pleasure, and his ache to be inside her approached unbearable. His desire for the woman in his arms was too great. How did he ever think he could live without her?

He lifted himself and moved to lie beside her. Brushing a stray lock of long black hair from her face, he saw the blush of satisfaction on her cheeks. He would love her for a lifetime. Like a torch, her hand burned when she laid it on his chest and directed him onto his back. The moment she gracefully moved over him, he thought he would explode. His desire vibrated with anticipation when she brushed it with her wetness.

Positioning herself so they touched in just the right place, she leaned down and kissed the patch of hair that rested in the center of his chest. Her actions told him she wanted him as badly as he did her.

He gritted his teeth. She was driving him crazy. He needed to fill her with his love. Then she pressed downward and buried every inch of his passion inside her.

She leaned her head back, and he heard the moan that

came from deep within. She was incredible, and she was going to make his pleasure peak if he didn't stop her. He placed his hands on her hips and held her firmly in place. "Don't move." Damn, she was beautiful. Her amber eyes sparkled in the dim light, and he knew they reflected love.

"Oh, really?" she said, then wiggled her bottom.

He gazed up at her. Her face held the look of mischief. "Don't tease me, I'm warning you."

"You're warning me? I think I have the upper hand in this situation."

Her beautiful smile warmed his heart. "That you do, Sam. That you do."

Seconds past until he felt he could release his grasp. When she slowly began to move again, he knew she was testing his control and he smiled. Her satin skin excited him causing his blood to surge through his veins, filling his heart with Samantha.

With one hand, he traced down her soft flat tummy and found her point of pleasure. The rapture on her face grew with heightened urgency as she teeter-tottered atop him.

She was close to total satisfaction. He believed her natural beauty had reached its zenith, but she was even more radiant in the heat of passion.

Meeting her steamed gaze, he continued to rotate his touch on her small sensitive crest. Memories of the first time they made love had been burned into his mind, but he didn't remember it being anything close to this. Then again, he loved her more now than ever.

He thrust deep within her, withdrew then pushed inside her again and knew he complied with her pleading movements when a burst of warmth drowned his passion.

Her contracting muscles surrounded him and squeezed his length. He was out of control. His own fuse ignited and exploded. Unable to stop the groan that came from his throat, he took her sweet lips in a kiss as he filled her with the burst of his love.

Slowly the tension left his body, and he looked up at the woman he cherished in all her beauty. His love for her was more than he could describe, so he wouldn't try. Surly his actions had said it all.

Ragged breathing filled the charged air. He was oblivious to the world beyond the four walls that encompassed them.

Samantha relaxed against him and he smiled to himself. His heart's rhythm slowed gradually then steadied.

Wanting to saver this very special time, he held her against his chest for a moment before gently lifting her off of him. He listened to her yielding sigh and cradled her to his side. Being with her was right. He knew in his heart she was the only woman he would ever truly love.

Sunlight filtered through the window and rested on Luke's disorderly hair. Samantha ran her fingers through the soft locks and pushed the tendrils away from his face.

She was looking at the man of her dreams. Her love for him was so great it couldn't all fit in her heart. It overflowed into her blood, her soul. She was possessed with it.

Sense the day she arrived at the ranch, she had longed for this moment. But what would happen now? Would they go back to their old lives? Each of them on the road, alone?

Why did she keep thinking that far into the future? The present was the most important thing and she was going to cherish every minute of it.

Luke's lids drifted open. The gray color of his eyes looked as if an artist had painstakingly painted each fleck of silver and black to perfection.

"Good morning," he said.

"Morning."

He pulled her to him. "You feel good. I like waking up

with you beside me."

She snuggled into his warm embrace. She loved waking up with him and wished it would go on for a lifetime. His naked body pressed against her, his shielding arms around her. It was a fantasy come true.

He kissed her forehead. "Hey, I'm starving."

Thoughts of food hadn't entered her mind, but now that he mentioned it. "Me too. Want to go into town for breakfast?"

"Sammi," He gazed into her eyes. "I don't mean for breakfast. I mean for you."

The evidence of his hunger was pressed against her thigh. Her passion began to bud. "Then, I guess you'd better sate your appetite." The huskiness of her own voice surprised her.

"Are you sure you wouldn't rather have some food?"

She answered with a kiss hungry for love.

CHAPTER 18

The sun hung above the hilltops. It had been a beautiful morning, and the afternoon promised the same. Life was beautiful and Samantha felt beautiful. She'd spent the last two days in Luke's arms.

She leaned against the deck rail and watched her mother and Howard get out of their car. The fairy tale was over, and all would get back to normal; but the fable would be written on the pages of her mind forever. She was sure she'd read it a million times.

Lena followed Howard onto the porch. Her eyes sparkled with love. Samantha was proud her mother would spend the rest of her life with the man she loved. She only wished she could.

"Hi, honey. How are you?" Lena kissed her daughter's cheek.

"Fine, Momma. Did you have a good time?"

"Wonderful."

The glance her mother shot her husband reflected the love the couple shared. She read it in Howard's eyes as well. "How about you...Daddy?"

Howard laughed. "Damn, I've been almost fifty-seven years without having a kid. Now, all the sudden, I've got two. I'd say someone upstairs dealt me a winning hand."

He kissed his wife. "To answer your question, Sam, I had the time of my life."

She watched Howard disappear through the doorway into the house. "Sit down, Mom."

"Just for a minute. I have a thousand things to get caught up on around here."

"Oh, relax. It'll all still be there in an hour." Samantha led the blushing bride to a chair and insisted she sit. Taking a seat next to her mother, she smiled.

"That's what I'm afraid of." Lena glanced around. "Where's Luke?"

"In the barn. He has a couple of horses he wants to break today."

"How's he getting along with that black stallion?"

"Slick? They were made for each other." Lena's expression took on that motherly look. She knew it meant personal questions were going to fly.

"And, how is he getting along with my daughter?"

Oh, how she loved this petite Indian woman. She couldn't stop the smile that lifted her lips. "Fine, Momma."

"Did you two talk while we were gone?"

Yes, if you could call lovemaking for hours on end talking. "Talk? About what?"

"Oh, Sammi. It was obvious at the party sparks were flying between you two."

"If you mean, did we talk about us, a future together, love, no." After the last two days, she had no doubt he loved her and her devotion to him was enormous. That's why she had to shield him from her past. She'd come to terms with killing her father, but what if... She wouldn't go over it in her mind again.

Now was as good a time as ever to break the news of her plans. "However, I made a decision while you were gone."

"About what, honey?"

She took hold of her mother's hand. "I'm going back

to work. My agent called and I'm booked in Laughlin starting Monday."

Disappointment filtered into Lena's eyes. "Oh, Sam."

"I know, Momma, but I have to." She glanced up as Luke led a horse out of the barn and into the corral. His masculine moves took her breath. She wanted to run to him and confess her love, but she couldn't take the chance. She'd already let it go too far. "I can't stay here."

"But, honey, Luke's going to stay. Why can't you?"

Couldn't Lena see he was the very reason she had to leave? "Mom, you don't know if he's going to stay or not." She studied Luke's skilled actions as he rode the bucking horse. "Look at him. He was made to rodeo."

"Looks to me like he's rodeoing right now. He just doesn't have a crowd watching him." She looked into her daughter's eyes. "You don't have to be on the road to do the things you love."

She couldn't argue. She'd love nothing more than to build a log cabin on the land Howard gave her. A recording studio would go nicely in a soundproof basement. But right now, she could only dream. "Okay, Momma, you win. Although, I still have to go."

Lena patted Sammi's hand and stood. "You do what you have to do." She nodded her head toward Luke. "But that man out there loves you. And you love him. Don't let years go by, like Howard and I did, before you figure it out. Life's too short."

"I know." She knew her mother knew the real reason she felt she had to depart. Lena turned and went inside the house. The older woman was right. Life was too short. If she couldn't have Luke, why not enjoy the other things she loved? She got up. Right now, a nice long ride on Markie might clear her head.

The screen door creaked when she opened it, and she stuck her head inside the house. "Mom, I'm going for a ride. Be back soon."

"Okay, honey. Be careful."

"I will."

She closed the door, ambled past the corral and tried to get Luke's attention. The horse he was on continued to buck and tromp the ground, and she went unnoticed. Oh, well, probably for the better anyway.

Familiar smells of leather and animal wafted on the air in the barn. She approached the horse she loved so much. "Hi, Markie. Ready for a ride? We'll have to hurry if we're going to see the sunset from the ridge."

⚜

Luke stepped out of the shower and grabbed a towel. He'd been glad to see Howard and Lena, but he'd miss the personal time with Sammi.

He was going to tell her he loved her and wanted her to be his wife, but now it was too late. Lena had been the one to break the news of Sammi's departure to him. He didn't have to wonder why she'd made the decision to go back on the road. Her career was important, and he wouldn't get in the way of its growth.

Buttoning his shirt, he walked down the hallway to the kitchen. Lena stood at the stove. "Smells like fried chicken."

"You have a good nose, Luke." She placed another piece of battered poultry into the pan. "It'll be ready soon."

"Great, I'm hungry."

"I hope Sammi gets back in time to eat with us."

"Where'd she go?"

"One of her favorite things is to ride up to the north ridge and watch the sunset."

"The north ridge?" A lump formed in his throat. "That's where she got shot at. How long has she been gone?"

"About an hour I guess. The sun has just barely gone

down. She should be back anytime."

"Why the hell didn't she tell me she was going?" The ashen color of Lena's face said his reaction scared her.

"Luke, do you think she's in danger?"

He drew a deep breath. "Probably not. It's been almost two weeks since anything's happened." He put his arm around the older woman. "Don't worry. We'll give her fifteen more minutes. If she's not back, I'll go find her. Then I'm going to tan her hide for putting us through this."

Lena's color began to return to normal, but his worry only deepened. Samantha should have known better than to go out by herself, especially so close to dark. He'd have to do something he couldn't just wait around.

Standing next to Markie, Samantha studied the western horizon. The pink and orange sunset was beginning to fade against the darkness. "Beautiful, wasn't it, girl?" She patted the horse's neck and started to mount. "We'd better head back to the house before it gets completely dark."

She turned at the sound of footsteps behind her. The shadow of a man walking towards her made her realize how unprotected she was. Her spine stiffened and tension crawled up the back of her neck. "Who is it?" She squinted into the darkness. "What do you want?"

"It's me, Sammi, Coker Johns."

The constricted muscles in her throat began to relax. "Coke, you frightened me. What are you doing out here? More investigation?"

"Not exactly."

He acted peculiar, and she didn't like it. "No? Then what?" She attempted to back away when he approached, but Markie stood behind her.

"You don't know how long I've waited for this."

Why was he being so weird? "Waited for what,

Coke?"

"For you to come to the ridge at sunset. Every evening for almost two weeks I've camped out and waited."

As quick as a rattlesnake strike, he grasped her arm. "What are you doing?" She tried to tear free of his grip. "You're hurting me." His cynical laugh caused her to tremble. Fear clutched her heart and her escalating pulse pumped blood swiftly through her veins. "Coke, what's wrong with you? Let me go."

"Sorry, I can't do that, Samantha. You're coming with me."

It felt as if his fingers ripped into her flesh when he pulled her toward the base of the ridge. Bile rose in her throat. Why was he doing this? "Where are you taking me?"

He snickered. "You'll find out soon enough."

Luke tightened the strap under Slick's belly. He glanced at his father who had a supporting arm around his crying bride. He studied Lena's tear-stained face. "She's probably just taking her time riding back, Lena. I'll find her."

His spirit lightened at the sound of galloping horse's hooves. "You see, there she is now." His life blood plummeted to the pits of hell when Markie appeared with no rider. "No!" He rushed to the mare and examined her for clues. "Damn, I wish you could talk, girl. Can you take me to her?" Markie whinnied and jerked her head back, then down, as if in answer. "Then do it, Markie. Let's go."

Time was futile. Samantha could be lying out there bleeding to death. He mounted Slick. "Lena, try to get hold of yourself. We need you. Call Johns, *now*. Tell him to get out here. Dad, gather the hands and form a search party." He turned Slick toward the barn door and grabbed Markie's loose rein. "I'll be back."

Sammi! He screamed her name in his mind, refusing to admit something had happened to her. He kicked Slick's sides. Riding away, the wail of a distraught mother echoed in his ears.

CHAPTER 19

Samantha twisted her wrists in a futile attempt to relieve the pressure of the handcuffs. Coker had been none too gentle when he wrenched her arms behind her back, shoved her against the patrol car and clamped the cold metal restraints tighter than necessary.

Time passed slowly. It seemed they'd been driving for hours, but she knew it had only been minutes. Coker had tied a bandana around her eyes. She scrunched her nose and tried to maneuver the black cloth away so she could see but it wouldn't budge.

Reasoning with the man was impossible. Her frustration mounted with his lack of response. "Coke, why won't you talk to me?"

She'd always liked Coker. Why was he doing this? It was impossible to analyze his actions. The years she'd known him had played over and over in her mind. There were no answers in their past or present that would indicate a motive.

"Coker, please. I thought we were friends." Damn his silence. "When you came to town, didn't we become friends? You told me you were interested in law-enforcement and I took you to the county courthouse and introduced you to everyone I knew."

She had done more than that, convincing Howard to put up most of the campaign money for Coke to run for Sheriff. "And why would you do this to Howard? He's been good to you."

"Good to me? That old man doesn't even know me. All my life I've wanted him to know *me*. Well, now he's going to," Coker growled.

She wondered what he meant. "What are you talking about?" She felt the car turn and heard the crunch of gravel under the tires. Tilting her head back, she tried to peek out from under her blindfold. If only she could get her bearings.

"Never mind." He stopped the car and turned off the engine.

"Where are we?" she asked. He grunted then got out of the car. The quiet inside the vehicle was deafening, but the silence was broken with each mashing footstep her abductor took on the loose rocks.

As soon as Markie got back to the house alone, Luke would start looking for her. How could she have been so stupid? Luke had warned her time after time not to go out alone, but she'd been too stubborn to listen and was paying the price. "Hurry, Luke," she whispered. "Hurry."

A welcomed rush of fresh air assailed her when Coker opened the door. She refused to plead with him any further. She'd be damned if she'd lose her pride to the likes of Coker Johns.

Sure to hold her head high, she stepped out of the car. He clenched her upper arm and pain shot into her shoulder.

"Come on."

He dragged her so hard she had to walk sideways to follow. Determined he wouldn't make her trip, with each stride she picked up her feet and put them down with confidence.

"Steps."

Silently, she counted as she went up. One, two, three,

four. Every detail could be important in her escape. Coke tapped on the door. The clicking sounds of a lock being worked from inside dissipated into the night.

"You made it."

The woman's voice was laced with relief. Samantha resisted the pressure of Coker's hand against her back. His shove propelled her forward and her boots slapped against a hard floor.

Her sensation of smell was heightened because of the blindfold. Cheap perfume, stale whiskey and cigarette smoke assaulted her nostrils. Each nasty odor made her stomach churn.

"I'll take her to the room. I've secured everything. She can't breakout. You'd better get back to your office. They'll be wanting the sheriff to come help them find their little Sammi."

Luke barged into the ranch house and headed for the study where he found Howard and Lena. "Is Johns on his way?" He glanced at the grandfather clock in the corner. "It's getting late. Where the hell is he?"

Howard stared at his son. "He wasn't there, but they radioed him. He'll be here shortly." He cleared his throat. "No luck?"

"Nothing. Not a trace. Markie led me straight to the north ridge, but..." He shook his head. "I've tried her cell several times."

Lena shook her head. She keeps it turned off while she's at the ranch."

"Dammit. Stands to reason. Are the hands ready?"

"They're horses are saddled. Each one of them is equipped with a flashlight and first aid gear. They have their cell phones, but with the bad reception we have around here, they might not work. All they're waiting for is a leader," Howard said.

The ring of the land line phone pierced the strained atmosphere of the room. Luke prayed it was Sammi.

Howard picked up the receiver. "Hello.

The older man frowned. "Coke said what?"

Luke wanted to yank the phone from his father's hand to hear personally what was being said on the other end. The look on Howard's face told him it wasn't good news.

"Dawn. That may be too late."

Luke's fury overwhelmed him. "The bastard's not coming, is he?"

Howard spoke away from the phone. "Not until morning."

He stomped out of the room. When this was over, he was going to kick that no-good sheriff's ass into the next county.

Samantha rubbed her wrists; thankful Coker had taken the cuffs off before the woman brought her in here and removed the rag from her eyes. She walked around the dingy, mid-sized bedroom then stepped into the small, attached bathroom looking for something, anything, to use as a weapon, but the woman had secured the place nicely. The windows having been boarded up and painted over, added to her despair.

Could they have been so stupid as to leave the door unlocked? She grasped the knob and turned. It didn't budge. What had she expected?

Even if she had her phone with her, they would have taken it away. It was a moot point now. All she could do was wait to see what happened.

"Luke, where are you?" The mattress sank beneath her, and the bedsprings squawked in protest to her weight. She lay back, closed her eyes and willed her mind to reach out to him. Now more than ever, she wished she were psychic.

Men and women's laughter filtered up from the floor below. Cigarette smoke seeped through the crack under the door.

Footsteps in the outer hallway caught her attention. The door lock clicked, and the buxom, middle-aged redhead that had removed her blindfold stepped into the room.

"How are we?"

"We? You're not a prisoner, Miss..."

"Call me Norma, honey."

"Call *me* Samantha." Norma? Could this be Norma's brothel? Luke said he'd seen Coker's patrol car here. There had to be a connection.

Norma set a tray on top of the dresser. "I brought you some food. It's getting late; I thought you might be hungry."

Her stomach churned and growled. She was ravenous. "Take it away." The woman's eyes were kind, but something behind them told Samantha she was not to be reckoned with.

"You may as well settle in and eat so you can keep up your strength. You're going to be here until we get what we want."

"What is it you want?"

"Just what Howard Hale owes me and my son. That's all."

"Your son?" Coker. It had to be. "Is Coke your boy?"

The woman reclaimed what she had brought in. "Are you sure you don't want this?"

She saw the color slowly wane from Norma's face. Bingo! "He is, isn't he?" One piece of the puzzle solved.

The black sky began to lighten in the east, and still no sign of Samantha. Luke knew there was no need for Johns to make a trip to the ranch. If she'd been on the property, he and the men would have found her.

"Let's call it a night boys and head back to the house. Thanks for your hard work. I want you all to take the day off and get some rest."

The new foreman rode his horse next to Slick. "If you need us, Mr. Dilashaw, we'll be there."

"Thanks, Gene. I appreciate it. And please, call me Luke."

"I'll do that."

The small legion trailed down the hill to the house. At least one good thing had come out of the ordeal. The men had accepted him and were willing to work for him.

They entered the barn as the sun peeked over the eastern vista. Luke figured the stallion was glad to be rid of his weight. "Gene, would you take care of Slick for me? I'm going to head into town."

"No problem, Luke."

He walked to the house and opened the door. The rich aroma of brewed coffee greeted him. He needed a good strong cup of the stuff.

"Hi, Lena." She turned and met his gaze. He watched the hope in her eyes vanish when she read his expression. "I'm sorry."

She returned her attention to the cups on the counter. "She's alive. I can feel it."

"Of course she's alive. And I'm going to find her." He stepped toward the tiny woman. He'd grown to love her. She'd taken him in as if he were her own. Being a new bride should have been one of the happiest times of her life. He vowed whoever was responsible for causing his new family this pain would pay.

"If you'll fix me a thermos of that good coffee of yours, I'll go into town and get that lazy sheriff off his butt."

Howard walked through the doorway. "Mornin', son. You look tired. Want me to go get Coke?"

His father's heart problems worried him. "No, thanks. You don't need any more stress. Rest, Dad, you'll need all your strength before this is over."

"You're right." He walked to his wife. "Besides, I think Lena needs me here."

Lena caressed her husband's cheek with a loving hand then handed Luke the thermos he'd requested.

"Thanks, ma'am."

She smiled. "You be careful now. You hear? I expect you to return with my daughter."

With a hug, he tried to lend her some of his strength. "I will, Lena. I will." He released her, took his phone from his pocket and checked the charge. Eighty-seven percent Good enough.

"If you hear anything, call me. You have my cell number. I'll have good reception in town."

"I sure will."

Luke went outside to his truck. What could be happening to Sam at that very moment haunted him. Was she being tortured, rap— "No!" He wouldn't let his imagination take him to that dark place. Bottom line, he would find her before anything like that could happen.

He turned off the lane and onto the road. At that time of morning, there was no traffic from the ranch into Lamoille and the miles went by fast. The tiny town was quiet, except for the neon sign lit over Idaloo's. Why hadn't he thought of Aaron Wiley?

He stomped on the brake pedal and the tires screeched against the pavement as he veered into the parking lot. He'd kill that little son-of-a-bitch if he had Samantha. Pulling to a stop at the back of the tavern, he saw a car parked by the door and wondered if it was Wiley's. Could the guy be stupid enough to be holding her here?

When his feet hit the dirt, he ran to the door. Pain shot through his knuckles when he pounded the hard surface. "Wiley, I know you're in there." He hammered against it again. "Wiley! It's Luke Dilashaw, open up." He heard a commotion inside and the door flew open.

"What the..."

Luke pushed passed Aaron Wiley. "Where is she?"

"Who?"

He whirled and grabbed him. "You jackass. Sammi." His glare was met by bloodshot eyes. Aaron Wiley's face was battered and bruised.

"What are you talking about? I—I haven't seen Sammi. You told me to stay away from her and I have. Please, Dilashaw, I'm telling you the truth."

Luke felt like the sniveling excuse for a man was indeed being truthful. He studied Wiley's face then released his grasp. "I'm going to look around anyway."

"Look all you want."

He turned and began to search the small saloon. Aaron followed him around like a puppy. "What the hell happened to you?"

"I got a little drunk last night and ticked off the wrong buckaroos."

Luke had a gut feeling Sammi wasn't there and hadn't been there. "I guess you won't do that again. Looks like they did a number on you."

"They did, and you're right, I won't."

After checking every corner of the building, Luke hurried to the door. He glanced at Wiley one last time. It was hard not to feel sorry for the poor man. "What are you still doing here?"

"I was afraid to leave. I thought they might be waiting for me."

"It's daylight now. I think it's safe for you to go home."

"Oh, I'm going home alright. Back to California. I

can't stand another minute of this redneck place."

Luke walked out the door. Wiley would be one less pain in the butt he would have to deal with. "Have a nice trip." He didn't care if he ever saw the Elvis look-alike again. His only concern was Sammi.

He drove off of the property determined to find the woman he loved and take her back to the H-H. Where he hoped she'd stay with him forever.

CHAPTER 20

Samantha stood in front of the dresser. Finally, the traffic in the hallway outside the room where she was being held prisoner, subsided. She had listened to the commotion all night and came to the conclusion she was for sure hostage at Norma's brothel.

It surprised her Coke Johns' mother was a prostitute. It didn't make any difference to her, everyone had to make a living, but she seemed to remember Coke telling her his parents were dead. The man was quite a liar.

She glanced at her watch for the umpteenth time. It had been almost twelve hours since the beautiful sunset. Funny what small things could entertain a person. She only wished she were outside so she could witness the dawn as well.

Heavy footsteps sounded in the corridor. The dead-bolt snapped, and the door opened. Coker stood in the entrance. His mere presence repulsed her.

"Good morning, Sammi. Sleep well?"

"What do you care?" She glanced in the mirror and cringed at the dark circles that had formed under her eyes.

He slammed the door. "Don't get pissy."

When he advanced toward her, she thrust her chin forward and resisted the urge to back away. His smile resembled the look of a cat who just ate a mouse. Her fear fought to surface, but she refused to let him know he scared her. "What do you want?"

"Do you have to ask?" He undid his belt buckle, took the gun holster off and laid it on the table by the door.

Her imagination didn't have to tell her what he planned. He popped the button on his trousers and slowly unzipped his pants. Her stomach churned. "Coker, don't do this."

"I've wanted you for a long time. It's time I had you."

Panic choked her. She glanced at the gun on the table. If only she could get past him.

"I see where you're looking. Don't get any ideas." He stopped in front of her. "Just relax and enjoy it. Fight me and you'll get hurt."

His breath smelled of whisky. "Think about what you're doing."

"Oh, I have been thinking about it. For years I've been dreaming about this very moment. Now, take off your clothes and lay down."

She couldn't let this happen. "No." The back of his hand landed hard against the side of her face. The blow forced her to turn her head to the side. Stinging heat penetrated her cheek. Pain shot through her jaw to her ear. She bit her lip and fought the tears that threatened to spill. She wouldn't give him the satisfaction.

Realizing she'd been holding her breath, she let the caged air escape. Slowly she rotated her head around and glared at her abuser.

Electrified silence filled the room. Coker grabbed her and threw her on the bed. He dropped on top of her and struggled to undo her jeans. His weight crushed her chest. She strained to inhale. His rough palm scratched her belly when he slipped his hand inside her pants. She swallowed to keep down the bile that stung her throat.

With all her strength she pushed against him, but her

attempt was useless. He worked his hand down farther, closer to her most private place. She clenched her teeth and forbid herself to cry out.

"Coke! What the hell do you think you're doing?"

Before he could answer, Sammi felt air rush into her lungs when his weight was lifted from her. Her eyes widened when she saw that Norma had grabbed him. She thanked God for his mother's one shred of decency.

"Momma, I..."

"Shut up! What the hell's the matter with you? Is your brain in your zipper? Do up your pants." She waited for him to dress. "Here, shut her up too."

Sammi sat up and watched Norma hand him a role of thick, gray tape, then walk to the table beside the door. The woman took his gun out of the holster. Her pulse pounded in her ears as she looked down the barrel of a Glock. What was going on?

She heard the tear of the tape separating from itself. Coke ripped the piece off and slapped it across her mouth. The adhesive pulled at her skin with the slightest movement.

"Now put the handcuffs on her," Norma demanded.

It was strange that Coker didn't argue with his mother, or show anger that she'd stopped him.

"Stand up, Sammi." He retrieved the cuffs. "Put your clothes on before I do this."

She quickly fastened her jeans, still thankful that Norma had interrupted his invasion.

"Turn around and put your hands behind your back."

The cold metal circles wrapped around her wrists.He snapped them shut then tightened them down until they dug into her flesh. His hard shove knocked the breath out of her. She went face first onto the bed. Whirling onto her back, she kicked at the culprit.

Coke smiled down at her. "Ha, ha. You missed."

Keeping the gun trained on Samantha, Norma slapped

his arm with her free hand. "You don't have the sense God gave a goose. Stop playing with her! We've got problems."

"What's up?"

"Luke Dilashaw's downstairs. He's asking for you."

⊱ ⊰

"Mmm, honey, you're one good looking cowboy. You sure I can't help you with something?"

Five women circled Luke like vultures waiting for a feast. There was a time when he would have enjoyed the attention, but not since Sammi came into his life. "Thanks, but I'm waiting for the sheriff."

"He's upstairs playing with his private stock. It might be a while," said another.

"We'd love to help you pass the time," remarked a blonde.

Instead of his winter Stetson, twirled his summer straw hat in his hand. "Ladies, I'm here on business." What the hell was taking Johns so long?

"It's your business we're interested in," one of the vultures said and grabbed his crotch.

"That's enough!" Coker entered the room. "You girls leave Mr. Dilashaw alone."

Luke saw Johns' clothes were twisted in disarray. It was obvious what had kept him. "Sorry I interrupted," he sneered. The hell he was. He couldn't believe the man had his own 'private stock', as the woman had called it.

Coker walked to the front door. "Let's get out of here."

He followed the sheriff outside. Even from the back, the man looked haggard, but he had no pity for him, only disgust. He grabbed the bastard and spun him around. In the early morning light, he caught the glint of small beads of sweat above Coker's top lip. "Why the hell didn't you come out to the ranch last night? Sammi's in trouble."

"The problems at the H-H aren't the only ones in Elko

County, Dilashaw."

How could this guy be so stupid? "You think drinking and visiting a whore house is doing your job? I'd say you're the one with a problem." He watched Johns straighten his uniform shirt and tuck it deeper into his pants.

"How did you find me?"

"I went by your office; they said you were 'out' for the night." He refrained from smashing his fist into the man's nose. "I've seen your car parked here before. I gambled, it paid off. Are you ready to go to work?"

"Yes. You're right. I apologize. I should have been there last night, but I had confidence you could handle the situation." He straightened. "Let's go to my office. You can tell me the details, and we'll start looking."

It was as if another person had jumped into Johns' body. He studied the sheriff's uniform. It was missing a very important part. "Where's your gun?"

"Oh-ah, I—I left it at the office."

Something about this wasn't right, but now wasn't the time to try to figure it out. He had to find Sammi. "Let's get going."

Sammi quivered and hope poured into her. Luke was there to get her. She knew he'd find her. A knock sounded at the door. She jerked her head up and prayed it was him.

Norma held the gun steady as she backed across the room to the door. "Who is it?"

"It's Connie. He's gone."

Sammi's heart sank. Gone, he couldn't be.

Norma lowered the gun. "Are you sure?"

"Positive."

The redhead turned and opened the door. A young woman with the same color of flaming locks, walked in.

Norma lifted the holster off the table, placed the gun inside and held the pair to her bosom. "Did you deliver the note?"

"Yes, Momma."

Momma? Coker had a sister? How many people were involved in this conspiracy?

"Good, girl. Here's a key to those cuffs. Take them off her and remove the tape."

When Connie jerked the bond from her mouth, Samantha felt like her flesh had been ripped away. She stood and met Norma's fixed gaze. "Tell me why you're doing this. I've never done anything to you. Hell, I don't even know you."

"Howard Hale knows me!" she spat. "And you've done more to me than you know, but that Luke Dilashaw, he's the one who's hurt us the most."

The handcuffs clicked and the tingling sensation in her fingers subsided. She rubbed her irritated wrist's. "What does Luke have to do with this? He's only been here a short while."

"Long enough to inherit the H-H. He doesn't deserve it. That ranch belongs to—"

"Momma! Don't tell her."

Samantha glared at the young woman. "Why not? Who can I tell? I'm a prisoner."

Norma sighed. "You're right, Connie." She turned the knob and pulled the door open. "I'll bring you some breakfast, Sammi."

She exhaled the breath she'd been holding. She'd almost found out what was behind this madness. Not that it would do her any good. "Don't bother. I'm not hungry." She watched Norma step through the gateway to the outside world and longed to be on the other side.

"Suit yourself. I'm not going to beg you to eat." She turned her attention to her daughter. "Come on, Connie, we need to get some rest. It's going to be a long day."

After the two crimson haired women walked out and slammed the door, she heard the thud of the deadbolt. Alone again. Only moments ago, Luke had been just a few yards away, but it may as well have been miles.

She went into the tiny bathroom. The cool water eased the sting the tape had left on her cheeks. Images of Luke streamed through her mind. She knew he'd be back.

CHAPTER 21

Luke took a chair in front of Coker's desk. Johns opened a drawer and took out a gun and holster that didn't look like the one the man usually wore. He'd never seen a law enforcement officer leave his weapon at the office. This guy was strange. There was something about him that didn't set right. How he got elected to office he didn't know

Coker sat behind the desk. "I'll call the deputies and have them head out to the north ridge."

It seemed the sheriff was always a step behind. "I've already had my men up there looking for leads."

Johns shrugged. "They won't find anything."

A strange confidence rang in Johns' voice and Luke didn't like it. "Pardon?"

"I—I mean," Coker shifted, "they're...not trained. My men are experts in finding clues."

One second, he was overconfident, the next he was a babbling idiot. It was amazing what staying up all night would do to a man. "You know what, Sheriff? I think you need some rest." He stood. "Send your men out and let them take a look around. I'll go back to the ranch and see if my father has learned anything. You get a couple of hours sleep, then give me a call."

Without giving Johns a chance to reply, he walked out. For some reason he could tell the man wasn't going to be of much help. He was showing a disinterest he'd never revealed before.

He had always thought Coker strange. How he got elected to public office, Luke would never know. Even with past difficulties, he had the feeling the sheriff's actions were merely a token effort to keep his position. One thing for sure, he wouldn't let his anger with Johns get in the way of finding Samantha.

"A what?" Luke's heart pounded as he took the paper from his father.

"It was in the mailbox down by the road. Someone must have put it there during the night."

The letters on the ransom note were identical to those on the previous two messages. "Who found this?"

"I did. Just a few minutes ago."

Luke read the words.

DO AS WE SAY AND THE WOMAN WON'T GET HURT. WE WANT ONE HALF OF A MILLION DOLLARS IN SMALL, UNMARKED BILLS. YOU HAVE UNTIL 7:00 p.m. TONIGHT. WE'LL CONTACT YOU WITH FURTHER INSTRUCTIONS.

Howard picked up the phone. "I'll call the bank."

If it meant losing everything he had in life, Luke would give it up just to hold Sammi in his arms again. "Do whatever you have to, Dad. I'll have Gene set up lookouts around the property. After you finish with the bank, call Johns. Ask him to order a phone tap."

He folded the note and put it into his shirt pocket. "There's more than one person involved."

"How do you know that?"

"The note referred to 'we'. Maybe we'll get lucky and somebody will botch their part of the plan."

Howard began to dial. "Let's pray for a miracle."

Luke heard someone enter the study. He turned to see Lena, her eyes filled with apprehension.

"Any news?"

Did she know about the note? Luke shot his father a questioning glance. The shake of Howard's head and his expression told the answer. Apparently, the older man didn't want his wife placed under more stress than necessary. "Not yet." Luke positioned his arm around her shoulder. "Let's get some fresh air." Not wanting her to overhear Howard's conversation with the bank, he led her outside to the deck.

"Did you see Coker?"

He guided her to one of the chairs. "Yes. He's sending someone to look around."

Tears streamed down her face. "My poor baby girl. I couldn't live if something happened to her."

He couldn't either, but he wouldn't allow himself to think negative. He knelt in front of her. "We'll find her. She's going to be all right. I'll stake my life on it." Her eyes were red and puffy when she looked at him.

"You love her too, don't you?"

It was time to lay everything on the table. "Yes. More than anything."

She put her arms around his neck and hugged him. "I knew it. I know you won't let anything happen to her."

"No, Lena, I won't." He gently backed away from her embrace. "Now relax. I know it's hard, but try." He stood, turned and started toward the bunk house. The sound of the little Indian woman's voice stopped him.

"Thank you, son."

Her words warmed his soul. Now he was her stepson, soon he hoped to be her son-in-law.

⤳⤶

"Coker, what got into you this morning?" Norma asked.

"Oh, Momma, I just wanted to have a little fun."

"Well, we'll be having plenty of fun when we get to Mexico. Besides, there are six girls working for me. You can have them anytime you want."

"I've had them all already. It's not the same. Sammi's...well, she's different."

"You could have ruined everything, you horny little bastard." She approached him and slapped his face.

He rubbed his cheek. "What'd you do that for?"

"It's an advance warning. Stay away from that girl."

"But, Momma..."

She leaned over and glared at him. "Don't you 'but Momma' me. I will not let your sexual fantasies be our downfall. Do you understand?"

He nodded.

"Good. We've waited your whole life for this." She straightened. "We're not getting the ranch like we planned, but I can live with five hundred thousand dollars. And I won't let you cause suspicion."

"I've pulled this charade off for a while now. I think I can do it for a few more hours."

"You'd better. When we're through with Howard Hale, he'll know what he did to me twenty-nine years ago." She looked at Coker. "If we did get the ranch, it would probably go under. You could never fill that man's shoes."

"Thanks for your confidence, Momma. I'm just as much a man as Howard Hale or Luke Dilashaw."

"If you believe that, my son, you'd better start acting like a sheriff. You've slipped back into your old skin lately. Buck up. Be the man you say you are. Your sister and I will take care of things around here. Now go on. And don't come back 'til it's time to let Samantha go. I don't want to take the chance of Luke coming here again."

"What if there's a problem and I need to come back?"

"We'll cross that bridge when we come to it. Call my cell. Go on, get out of here."

"Yes, ma'am."

⚬❦⚬

Luke watched the sheriff's car pause by the mailbox before continuing up the lane.

Coker stopped the car and got out. "I brought you something." He went to the rear of the vehicle and opened the trunk.

Luke walked over and peered in. "Walkie-talkies. Good." Maybe Johns was going to come through after all. Luke wondered if he'd given the man a fair shake.

"I thought your lookouts could use them."

"How many are there?"

"Twenty."

Luke bent, lifted the box of black communication devices and took them to the table on the deck. "We're in luck. There's the foreman now." He motioned to the man on horseback. "Gene, come here."

Gene reined the horse to a halt. "Yes, sir?"

"Since our cells aren't of much use in the mountains, Sheriff Johns brought us walkie-talkies. Fill your saddlebags with them and distribute them among the men."

"Be glad to. I was just fixing to make a round."

"Thanks, Gene." He directed his attention to Coker. "Let's go take a look at that ransom note." Luke led the way into the house.

"Dilashaw, about this morning."

He didn't want to hear the man's *true confessions*. It was none of his business who he slept with. "Don't worry about it." He entered the doorway to the study. "Let's concentrate on finding Samantha."

"I just want you to know that doesn't happen very often. Sometimes the stress of this job gets to me, and I..."

Luke faced him. "Look, I don't care about your private life. All I care about is Sammi's safety. You're here now, so let's get to work."

"You've got it. Where's this note?"

"Right here." Luke unfolded the paper and handed it to the sheriff.

"You say Howard found this?"

"In the mailbox."

Coker studied the page. "I stopped on the way up. Nothing's there now."

"I have a man watching the box; the others are in key areas."

"I don't think they'll come to the ranch."

How would the man know if they would come to the ranch or not? "They entered the property to kidnap Sammi in the first place."

"Well, that's different. They had to get their prey. That part's over, and now they want their money. Did you get the half million they're asking for?"

"Yes. What do you think their next move will be?"

"Like they said. They'll contact you about delivering the money and returning Sammi."

"When are they going to come put the tap on the phone?" He glanced at the clock on the wall. "We only have a couple of hours."

Coker took a seat. "They should be here soon. What makes you think the kidnappers are going to call? Why not send another note?"

"They can't be stupid enough to think we won't have high security. How would they deliver it?"

"That stands to reason. Well, in any case, the tappers will be here anytime. Where's Howard and Lena?"

"Right here, Coke," Howard said as he entered the room, Lena following.

Luke offered the woman a chair. "Did you two get any rest?"

Lena sat down. "As much as we could." She glanced up at Luke. "Anything?"

Her strained look stole his heart. He shook his head and glanced up at the sound of Johns' voice.

"I wish you folks would relax. Sammi's going to be alright. She'll be back with you soon. I guarantee it. I'm doing everything I can to see to it."

The man's words were ones of comfort, but his tone was too nonchalant for Luke. What little faith he had in the sheriff was fading fast. The man shifted, too often, and he wouldn't look any of them in the eye. He knew there was something he wasn't telling.

Lena took Coker's hand. "I believe you will, Coke. Between you and my son, I know nothing will happen to my baby girl."

Howard sat behind his desk. "I've told Lena everything, so we can talk freely in front of her. Luke, did you put the money in the safe?"

"Yes, sir. You were sleeping when the banker arrived, so I took the liberty. He said the bills aren't marked, but he wasn't pleased about it. When I deliver the cash, I'll do everything not to let the kidnappers get away with it."

Howard frowned. "Now don't go putting yourself in danger. That money can be replaced. You and Sammi can't."

Luke agreed with his father, and he didn't give a damn about the money. As long as Sammi was safe. "You're right. I'll take Sammi and run. They can have their blood money."

Coker cleared his throat. "Now, Dilashaw, I can't let you deliver anything. My position won't allow it. I'll do it myself."

"The hell with your position. My position is this; if it's in my power to get Samantha to safety, I'm going to do it, and you're not going to stop me." Did Johns think he was just going to stand around and do nothing?

Coker stood. "Luke, I know you're upset, but don't forget, I'm trained in such matters."

Luke stepped closer to the sheriff. He wanted to wipe the man's superior look off his face with his fist. "When was the last time you handled a kidnapping in Elko County?" Coker had no answer. "That's what I thought. I'm not putting Sammi's life into your hands."

"Don't mess with the law, Luke. It's for your own protection as well as your family's."

Lena stood and stepped between the two men. "Luke, please, this isn't helping things."

Damn he couldn't wait until this was over so he could deal with Johns on a personal basis. He realized the stress over Samantha had his emotions on a roller coaster, but he didn't like Johns. This wasn't the time to confront him.

If the law forced him to let the sheriff handle this, then he'd do it, but he wouldn't be far behind. He didn't understand why his suspicion of the man grew with each passing moment.

CHAPTER 22

Sammi sat quietly on the bed. It had been twenty-four hours since they'd brought her here. What else could she do but wait?

She knew she'd have to give in and eat, her stomach protested its emptiness, and Norma was right, she did need to keep her strength.

An abundance of activity had gone on outside her door all afternoon. It sounded as if the people involved were moving. The silence that carried through the walls now seemed to confirm her notion.

It only made sense that Norma wouldn't be able to stay in business in Elko. She wondered what they were asking in return for her, and when she'd get to go back to her family. *If* she got to go back. Fear stabbed her like a knife. She knew who they were. Could they afford to let her live? Being cooped up inside this room made her crazy, she had to learn her fate.

The sound of her growling stomach filled the quiet room. She rose, walked to the door and pounded against the hard surface. "Hey, anybody there? Hello! Norma?" Placing her ear against the cool wood, she listened. Hearing footsteps coming up the stairs, she stepped back and waited for the door to open. Amazement struck her when she realized she was actually glad to see the red-haired woman.

"What is it, Sammi?"

She wanted to say this just right. "Norma, I'm sorry I haven't accepted your hospitality and eaten the food you've brought me. Is it too late to change my mind?"

Norma smiled. "Not too late at all, but you don't have to suck up to me. What is it you really want?"

She should have known Norma would see through her ploy. "I want to know when I'm going home."

"It won't be long now. The end is near. What time does that watch of yours say?"

Sammi glanced at the face of the time piece. "A quarter to seven."

"I'd say there's enough time to get you a bite to eat." Norma started out the door.

Samantha instinctively reached for the older woman's arm. "Wait! You haven't told me anything."

Norma yanked free of Samantha's grasp. "Don't worry, a couple more hours and you'll be free."

"Then you do plan to let me go?"

"Of course, we're not killers, you know. We just want what's rightfully ours." She walked out and locked the door.

"And what could that be?" Sammi whispered, hoping against hope Norma was telling her the truth.

Luke had clenched his jaws for so long his teeth were beginning to ache. This waiting was driving him mad. He looked at the clock on the wall. "It's five minutes to seven. Where the hell are those phone guys?"

Coker stood and walked to the desk. He picked up the telephone receiver. "I'll call the office and see if they know anything."

He battled to control his temper. "It's a little late for that isn't it? I've been asking you to do as much for the last hour."

Coke placed the apparatus back onto its cradle. His hand rested on its back. "You're right. I should have called earlier."

Luke was disgusted because he was supposed to trust this man with Sammi's life, and he didn't. He approached and stood face to face with the sheriff. "Johns, I've got one nerve left and you're getting on the damn thing. When this is over, I'm—" The ring of the phone silenced him. His pulse rate doubled in a split second. This was it.

Coker's hand still on the receiver, he lifted it to his ear. "Hello."

Had this whole scene over the telephone been a ruse so Coker could answer the call? He wished there was another extension. He wanted to know what the kidnappers had to say. Silent, he, Howard and Lena sat in anticipation.

"Yes, we've got the money.

"In one hour? Where?

"Is Samantha alright?

He met Coker's gaze. "I want to talk to her."

Coker shook his head from side to side.

What did he mean no? "Son-of-a-bitch, you tell them I want to talk to her, and do it now. If I don't hear her voice, no money!" He prayed this wouldn't jeopardize her further, but he had to know she was okay.

"I'll be there in an hour, but first we want to talk to Miss Rainwater."

Luke glared at him. "Not *we*, me."

"I understand."

Luke spoke up. "I mean it, no money."

"Look, I can't help it, Dilashaw's insisting. Just go get her."

Luke read something in Johns' tone, but he couldn't quite grasp what it was. The seconds that passed seemed like hours as he waited to speak to the woman he loved.

"Hold on." Coker handed Luke the phone.

Samantha had just taken the last bite of the sandwich Norma brought her, when the woman stormed into the room. Her cheeks were flushed and her eyes held a blaze of anger. Coker's thirty-eight rested in her palm.

"Get off your butt and come with me."

She stood. "What is it? What's happened?"

"Dilashaw's on the phone. He wants to talk to you."

The air rushed out of her lungs. "Luke? He knows I'm here?"

"He has no idea where you are. Now listen to me. I told you earlier we're not killers, but don't underestimate that statement. If you try to send him any hidden messages, I'll blow a hole in you. Now take a hike down the stairs."

She had to think fast. How could she let Luke know where she was without alerting Norma? Think. Think. With each step, she heard the madam's footsteps close behind. At the bottom she paused. "Where's the phone."

"Straight through the door in front of you. Now move."

Her knees threatened to give way as she forced her feet forward. The closer she got to hearing Luke's voice, the more violent her trembling became. She had to calm down and gather her thoughts.

Connie held her hand over the mouthpiece of the telephone receiver. "Three words, Sammi. Luke, I'm okay. That's all you say. Understand?"

Sammi thought her heart was going to thump through its boundaries. She nodded. What would they do to her if she tried to say more? She glanced at the gun in Norma's hand and realized she couldn't take the chance. Stepping forward she reached for the phone.

Connie pulled it back. "I'll hold it. You talk."

She leaned forward and the young woman placed the cool plastic to her ear. "Luke?"

"Sammi, are you alright?"

She closed her eyes. His deep, smooth voice was calm. She wanted to hear more. A sharp jab into her side made her force her eyelids open. The expression on Connie's face told her she'd better answer. "Yes, I'm okay."

The young redhead jerked the receiver away and slammed it onto its cradle.

Sammi's emotions sank. Quick as a snap of her fingers it was over. Luke was gone.

Luke slowly put down the phone. "She's okay. For now." He watched his father rise and walk to his anguished wife.

"She'll be fine, Lena," Howard said. "Let's go to our room. You need to lie down. We'll let Luke and Coker handle this." He helped her stand and led her out of the room.

Luke turned to Coker. "What did they say?"

"They said to bring the money into town, and in one hour they'll call the sheriff's office with the drop off point."

This was insane. "Have you ever heard of someone calling the police station and leaving instructions to drop off ransom money?"

Coker frowned. "It happens all the time in the movies."

What kind of mentality did this man have? "Damn it, Johns, this is real, not Hollywood."

"I know it's real, Dilashaw. And yes, the law is often involved in ransom deliveries." He fidgeted with his gun. "Now, where's the money? I need to go."

"I'll be right back." He had to get away and mentally assemble all the happenings of the last few weeks. Something wasn't right.

He stepped out the back door, fresh air a welcome change from the stifling, claustrophobic atmosphere Coker created with his presence. Simply being away from the man cleared his mind.

He leaned against the door and closed his eyes, letting scenes play behind his lids. He tried to remember the smallest details of every event that had happened since the first threatening note.

In just moments, it was clear that suspicions of Coker Johns had been evident on every occasion. Even the voice at the pond, no wonder it sounded so familiar, it was Johns. The day at the sheriff's office when the man said he was in the men's room he must have been outside putting the note on the car. Johns was somehow involved in this whole thing. He didn't know what part the man played, but he knew he had to go along with the escapade in order to find out.

He went back inside the house, hands fisted at his sides, but for Samantha's sake he couldn't confront Coker now. When he rounded the corner of the doorway, Johns was sitting behind the desk. Funny, the man kind of resembled Howard. "Okay, Sheriff, I'll get the money."

Coker stood. "You mean you're going to let me have it?"

Luke could have kicked himself for not seeing through the ignorance this man sometimes showed. "Of course, why wouldn't I?" He walked to the safe.

"I—I don't know. I just thought you'd fight me."

"No, I've realized you're the best man for the job." He almost choked on the lie as he closed the heavy strongbox door. "This briefcase has half a million dollars in it." He handed it to Johns. "Guard it with your life. I know you'll do everything possible not to let the kidnappers get away with it." He watched the sheriff's eyes sparkle when his fingers wrapped around the handle like a child with a new puppy.

"I'll do everything, yes. I'd better go."

"Did I understand you correctly? You're going to your

office and wait for the next call, then you'll drop off the money and pick up Sammi?"

Coker clutched the case. "Right. You stay here. I'll call you when there's news."

"I'll wait by the phone." He took Coker by the arm. "Let me walk you out."

He escorted the sheriff outside to his patrol car. Johns treated the briefcase like a newborn baby when he placed it onto the passenger seat.

"I'll be seeing you, Dilashaw."

He probably wasn't supposed to recognize it, but Luke heard the finality in Coker's voice. "Yes, you will." How could he have gone so long without seeing through this man?

He watched him drive down the lane then hastened to the bunkhouse and stepped inside. The ranch foreman sat at a small desk nestled in the corner. "Gene, call all the men in. We've wasted enough of their time." He saw the questioning look that crossed Gene's face.

"What did you find out?"

"Let's put it this way, the sheriff's involved."

"Coker?"

He nodded. "Alert the highway patrol about the situation." He patted his pocket to make sure he had his cell. "I'll get in touch with them as soon as I need their help."

"Yes, sir."

Luke drove into town. He felt conspicuous in his truck. He should have thought to take Gene's. Someone honked and drew his attention. He glanced in the direction of the sound. "Johnny. Perfect timing," he mumbled, as he pulled into the casino parking lot where his uncle sat in his old clunker of a car. He parked next to the blue bomb.

"Luke, what brings you to town?" Johnny asked.

"Sorry, no time to waste. I need a favor."

"I'll help if I can. I owe you after what I did. What do you need?"

"To borrow your car."

"What's wrong with your truck?"

"Can't explain right now." He studied the battered body of the old Nova. "Is this thing in good running condition?"

"Hell yes. I got 'er souped up. She'll out run anything she goes up against."

Luke smiled. Johnny Hale was good for something after all. "Can I use her?"

Johnny took off his ball cap and scratched his head. "I guess so."

Luke touched the brim of his cowboy hat. "Can I use your cap too?"

"What's going on?"

He glanced at his watch. Damn, he was behind schedule. He'd have to level with him. "Look, Sammi's been kidnapped. I think I know who's got her, but if I use my truck, they'll recognize me."

Johnny moved away from the car door. "Hell, boy, what are you doin' wastin' time. Take her; and here's my cap."

Luke accepted the red ball cap and gave his uncle his cowboy hat. "Thanks, Johnny. I'll bring her to your house in the morning. I'm sure all this will be over by then."

"Don't worry about it. Just get Sammi. I know you love that gal."

Placing the cap on his head, he said, "More than life itself." He pushed in the clutch and power vibrated though the Nova when he started its engine.

Johnny shut the door. "Get outta here."

He drove out of the parking lot and straight to the sheriff's office. Circling the block, he saw no sign of the sheriff's patrol car. At the back of the building, he realized it wasn't there either. That bastard. Had he gotten away?

CHAPTER 23

Something in his gut told him to check Norma's. Whatever this feeling was, gnawed at him so fiercely, he couldn't ignore it. When he pulled the old blue Nova in front of the bordello, he saw his intuitions had been right. The back of Coker Johns' patrol car could be seen parked behind the two-story house. Lights from inside the structure illuminated the windows.

He wondered if Samantha was in there. His concern pounded deep within his chest. Waiting was the hardest part, but he had to remain in the car and see what Johns' next move would be.

In his rear-view mirror, he saw a set of headlights coming up the street and quickly slumped down. The car stopped directly behind the Nova. He watched in the side mirror as a man got out. Staggering into the back of the Nova the man cursed, rubbed his knee then continued to the door of Norma's brothel.

Luke heard the slight rapping sound as the drunk man knocked. Moments passed, and there was no answer. With his fist, he hammered again. Nothing. After his third attempt, he gave up and started back to the car.

Luke's heart sank to his feet. Was no one there? Where were they? He got out of the car and approached the front door. The drunk man walked toward him.

"Forget it, buddy, nobody's home."

His frustration mounted. "There has to be someone here. The sheriff's patrol car is parked in the back."

"The hell it is." The man took a few steps to the side and looked to the back of the house. "Hmm, that's strange. I thought I just saw the sheriff?"

Luke stopped dead in his tracks. "What did you say?"

"I just saw the sheriff in his own car."

"When?"

"A few minutes ago."

"Where?"

The man stumbled backwards. "Now let me see. Where was that?"

He wanted to shake the answer out of the guy. He suspected he wasn't as intoxicated as he appeared. "Think, man. Fast." As if a light bulb lit up in his brain, the man's eyes brightened, and Luke let out the breath he'd been holding.

"I know, he was heading out of town on old county road 120." He smiled. "Had a good-looking woman with him too. She wasn't one of Norma's, that's for sure. That long black hair. She looked like an Indian."

"Sammi!" He'd let Johns slip through his fingers. "Where is this county road?" He listened to the directions then ran to his car.

ॐ

Samantha sat in the passenger seat. She glanced at Coker as he took another swig of whiskey. He didn't even look like himself without his uniform on. But then, he wasn't the Coker Johns she thought she knew. "Why did you have to put these handcuffs on me again?"

He laughed. "You're a fighter. I couldn't take the chance of you opening the car door and jumping out."

"Why didn't you just leave me at Norma's?"

"Because I have plans for you."

The dim moonlight didn't stop her from seeing the sneer on his face. Just to think she had once trusted this man made her feel like a fool. "What plans?"

He chuckled. "Momma's well on her way to Mexico, Miss Sammi."

Her heart skipped a beat. "What are you going to do, Coker?"

"Don't tell me you haven't guessed." He glared at her. "You. I'm going to *do* you, but no one will stop me this time."

She was sure she was going to be sick. "Coke, stop please." Heat rushed to her face and her stomach rolled.

He whipped to the side of the road. "Don't puke in my car." He got out, ran around to the passenger side and opened the door.

The cool night air that rushed in relieved some of her nausea. She took some deep breaths and resisted the urge to throw up on Coker's shoes as he stood outside the door. "I'm a little better." Maybe if she got out, she could figure a way to escape. She glanced to the driver's side of the car. She had seen Coker put his gun under the seat, but it was impossible for her to get to it. "Can I walk around for a minute? I think it will help."

"Sure, get out, but first I'll have to take your boots off."

"Why?"

He shrugged. "I don't want you to get any ideas about running. It'll just waste time. You couldn't outrun me anyway."

There went that plan. A strange vibration traveled through her, and she felt she had to stall. Her life may depend on it. "Then take them off. I just want to get some fresh air and stretch my legs."

Coker hoisted her boots from her feet and set them in

the back seat. "This is perfect."

"For what?" She stepped out and stood beside the vehicle. If she was out of the car, she'd have a better chance of escape than if she was caged inside.

He went to the back of the car, opened the trunk and pulled out a blanket. "This," he said, and laid the blanket on the ground. "You know, I think we're far enough out of town that after we make love, I could let you go." He reached inside the passenger door. "Want some music?"

The sound of the radio blared in her ears. She glanced around. No cars in sight, no lights from far away houses, nothing. Only the moon, stars and miles of Nevada wilderness. It could be hours before someone drove this old highway. She drew a long, unsteady breath. Why?

Her stomach clenched into a tight knot. She stood on legs that wanted to run, if only to prolong the inevitable. Before she could force them into motion, Coker grabbed her, his fingers digging into her skin.

She tried to twist out of his grasp. "Let me go, you sorry..." Her head hit the hard desert floor, and pain penetrated her skull. Her arms ached when her weight smashed the handcuffs into her back and tightened their grip. Coker stood over her. If she had to fight to her death, she vowed he wouldn't have her.

His fingers grasped the zipper tab on his pants. With every ounce of strength, she drew her leg back and kicked his right ankle. His foot went out from under him, and he landed on the dirt.

"You little bitch!" He crawled to where she was and drew his hand back.

"No!" She rolled away and barely missed the blow intended for her jaw. A thousand little stings penetrated her skin when the sharp rocks poked her body. The handcuffs dug into her wrists when she rolled across them. The ground dealt no torment compared to what she suffered inside. She'd never been so frightened or out of control.

Each beat of her heart felt like a hammer, and the throb in her temples began to blur her vision. Her hands were numb, but she wouldn't give in. "Stay away from me, Coker!"

"You may as well stop this right now before you get hurt." He grabbed her shoulder. "Listen to the music and relax." He straddled her legs.

When she drove her knee into his groin, he crumpled to the ground in pain. She drew back her foot and heaved it into his groin. She had no sympathy when he grabbed himself, moaned and rocked from side to side. Hit twice in the same place should keep him down for a time.

She had to move. Turning on her side, she bent into a fetal position and thrust her cuffed hands around the underside of her bottom. Her muscles strained, the metal around her wrists cut deep as she brought her hands and arms to the front of her body. Now she could run. When she pushed herself off the ground, Coker's hand seized her ankle.

"You're not getting away that easy." He pulled her down. "I'll kill you for this, Samantha."

What was that noise? Was it her heart pounding so loudly it was causing her ears to hum? She listened intently, trying to hear around the blasting music on the radio. A car? Please let it be a car. When she looked up her stomach fluttered at the sight of headlights coming up the highway. She prayed they'd stop and help her. "You'd better kill me quick because I intend to fight you until the end."

"Not yet. You're going to be warm when I have you."

Maybe if she kept his attention, he wouldn't notice the vehicle until it was too late. "Okay. Then have me and get it over with." Closer and closer the lights came. Coker put his hand on her breast. She wanted to spit in his face, but help was only yards away.

Coker jerked his head up. "What's that?" He

scrambled to his feet.

Samantha stood. Coker resembled a deer frozen in place by the beam of a bright light. The car skidded to a stop. Still, Coker stared.

The driver's door flew open, and Samantha knew her prayers had been answered when Luke rushed toward her. As if poked with a cattle prod, Coker sprang into action. He sped past her and dove head first into the car. She knew what he was after. "Luke he's got a gun!" She grabbed Coker's feet and tried to pull him out, but she had no strength. In a scant second, Luke was by her side.

"Get out of the way, Sammi."

She backed up. Luke groaned as he grabbed Coker's ankles and jerked him out of the car. He landed on the ground with a thud. A scream welled in her throat when she saw Coker turn over and level the gun on Luke.

"Kiss your ass good-bye, Brother," Coker spat.

Luke didn't bat an eye. With one quick swipe of his foot, he kicked the gun out of Coker's hand. Sammi held her breath as it flew through the air.

Luke heard the weapon clatter to the desert floor a few feet away. He reached down, grabbed Johns by the collar and pulled the slime ball to his feet. "You son-of-a-bitch." He drew back his fist.

"No, wait!" Coker pleaded lifting his hands into the air. "I surrender."

It took all the restraint he could muster to fight the force that compelled him to land the blow anyway. Slowly he eased his arm down, keeping a close eye on Johns. "Sammi, you alright?"

"I'm fine. I've got the gun."

The simple sound of her voice eased his mind. He glared at the man in front of him. "I should kill you for putting her through this."

"You wouldn't want to kill your own brother, would

you?"

Luke shoved him against the car. "You bastard, I don't have a brother."

"Listen to me, Dilashaw, I am your brother. Your half-brother."

Luke swallowed hard. What the hell was he talking about? "I won't listen to your lies." He released his hold. "Sammi, keep that gun aimed at his head. If he tries anything, shoot." He glared into Johns' eyes. "She killed her own father. Don't think she'll hesitate to shoot your worthless ass." He only hoped his threat was a fact. That Sammi could indeed blow him away if she needed to.

Luke walked to the driver's side of Coker's car, relieved to find the keys in the ignition. He studied the ring and found the small key that would unlock Samantha's bindings.

He went to her side and whispered into her ear. "Are you okay with the gun?"

Her hands trembled. "Yes."

"Hold steady, while I unlock these cuffs." His heart sank when he saw the marks the restraints left on her wrists. "I'm going to put these on him, then you can put the gun down."

"If it's all the same, I think I'll just hold it."

"Whatever you want."

"Come over here, you bastard." Luke shoved Johns against the trunk of the car. "Put your hands behind you."

Coker placed his hands to the small of his back. "Luke, Howard Hale is my father. Why do you think I did this?"

How could the man continue with his lies when he knew they would do him no good? "Save your story for your defense attorney." he clamped the cuffs as tight as he could. "A taste of your own medicine."

He led Johns to Johnny Hale's car, opened the passenger door and shoved the man inside. "You're going to pay for this, Johns. On the way to town, Sammi will be in the back seat with that gun trained on your head, so don't try anything." Luke checked his pocket to make sure he had the ignition keys to the Nova. When he felt them, he slammed the door.

He turned. Samantha stood right behind him. The moonlight illuminated the twinkle of a tear creeping down her cheek.

"I knew you'd come."

He pulled her into his embrace. "I'm sorry I let this happen. I'll never let you out of my sight again."

"Never?"

He lifted her chin with his fingertips. His soul was filled with this woman. "Never. I love you."

"Oh, Luke."

His lips met hers and for that brief moment, all was forgotten, all but his need to make her his.

EPILOGUE

Luke studied his reflection in the mirror and straightened his tie. "I'm glad they caught Norma and her daughter. Another hour, they would have made it to Mexico, and you wouldn't have gotten your money back."

Howard walked up behind him. "Me too. I wonder why that woman never told me she got pregnant the night of the Elko rodeo? That was the night your mother left me. Can't say I blame her."

The image of the man beside him was what he'd look like in thirty some years. "I don't know, Dad."

"Norma used to be a good girl. At least I thought she was. Funny I never thought of her again after your mother left. Even when Norma's brothel went in, I didn't associate the two. She'd been gone for so long." He paused. "Now I find out I have another son."

Luke faced his father. "Let's not talk about it. The trial will be over soon, and we can get on with our lives. Coker's already said he didn't want anything to do with us, and we'd never be his family." He put his hand on Howard's shoulder. "I don't want anything to spoil this day."

"Oh, Momma, how do I look?" Sammi twirled in front of the full-length mirror. She never thought this day would come.

"Like a beautiful bride." Lena straightened the lace of Sammi's veil.

Her dreams had come true. She was going to be Mrs. Lucas Dale Dilashaw. "Are you sure everything's set for the reception at Idaloo's?"

Lena smiled. "Yes, baby girl, you've made me call three times. The young lady who bought it said everything is ready."

She took a deep breath. "I'm just so nervous." Checking her watch again, she realized it was only minutes before the ceremony would begin.

Her thoughts drifted to her valley and the log house she and Luke built next to the pond. "I can't believe the changes the last few months have brought." She met Lena's gaze. "Just think, I'm going to spend the night in a new home with my husband. Next week I have the first session booked in my very own recording studio. Luke has taken to running the H-H like a duck to water. Ida helped me plan my wedding, my mother is the matron of honor in my wedding, and my father's the best man."

Ida stepped through the door. "Lena, are you ready? Ben is waiting to escort you to the altar."

Lena hugged Samantha then pushed her to arm's length. "Speaking of which. It's time to walk down the aisle."

Samantha's muscles tightened and her pulse jumped into overdrive. She was about to marry the man of her dreams. She followed Lena and Ida out the door and into the lobby of the small church. Organ music drifted around her.

Ben held his arm out and Lena put hers through it. "Thank you, Ben."

The two left the foyer and Sam glanced through the doors into the chapel filled with friends and family. Her knees went weak when she saw Luke standing at the altar. The black tuxedo brought out the gray in his eyes and his straight white teeth gleamed beneath his neatly trimmed mustache. She longed to kiss his lips. Too handsome to be real, he was a fantasy come true.

"Sammi. Sammi!"

Ida's shouted whisper grabbed her attention. The wedding march was playing. She couldn't breathe, couldn't move. Luke held out his hand, inviting her to his side. The mere strength of his want for her forced air into her lungs and propelled her forward. Her gaze locked with his as she walked down the path to the future.

When she stopped before the three stairs, her husband-to-be stepped down. The tender touch of his hand on her elbow offered her support as she took the stairway to happiness.

She heard the minister when he spoke, but the love she saw in Luke's eyes penetrated her very essence, and the words faded into the background. Did she have the same effect on him? His tender look said it all. How could two people be so much in love?

Samantha saw the minister's hand come up from his side and touch Luke on the shoulder, at the same moment she felt him touch her as well. The man's voice came into focus.

"The rings, please." The pastor accepted the two plain gold bands from Howard then gave the larger one to her. "Repeat after me."

She completed her vows and waited while the chaplain handed the small ring to Luke.

"Repeat after me."

As she looked into Luke's eyes, the link of love encircled her finger. He held it in place, and his loving words brought her heart to a standstill.

"With this ring, I thee wed."

ABOUT THE AUTHOR

From her musical roots to her success as an author and entrepreneur, Sharon embodies the spirit of creativity and determination in the heart of the Ozarks.

In the 1990s, Sharon and her husband made the move to the beautiful Ozark Mountains. A talented musician by trade, Sharon continued to perform, but a new passion began to blossom: writing fiction.

Sharon's journey took an exciting turn when she joined Ozarks Romance Authors. This opened doors to new opportunities, including attending conferences and workshops. Immersing herself in the writing community, she honed her skills in both writing and navigating the dynamics of publishing.

Her dedication and hard work have resulted in a collection of **twenty-one published titles**! Her writing spans a diverse range of genres, including:

- Historical Westerns
- Contemporary Romance
- Contemporary Western Romance
- Mystery
- Short Stories
- Children's Books

Driven by a desire to support fellow writers, Sharon established Paperback Press, an indie author service company. She finds great joy in sharing her knowledge and expertise with aspiring authors, guiding them through the often-complex world of writing and publishing.

Today, Sharon continues to live in the Ozarks with her husband and their two dogs, Willie and Waylon.